THE LITTLE LAME PRINCE
AND
THE ADVENTURES
OF A BROWNIE

THE
LITTLE LAME
PRINCE

AND

THE ADVENTURES OF
A BROWNIE

BY DINAH MARIA MULOCK CRAIK
ILLUSTRATED BY LUCILLE CORCOS

ILLUSTRATED JUNIOR LIBRARY

GROSSET & DUNLAP
NEW YORK

THE LITTLE
LAME PRINCE

CHAPTER 1

Yes, he was the most beautiful Prince that ever was born.

Of course, being a prince, people said this; but it was true besides. When he looked at the candle, his eyes had an expression of earnest inquiry quite startling in a newborn baby. His nose—there was not much of it certainly, but what there was seemed an aquiline shape. His complexion was a charming, healthy purple. He was round and fat, straight-limbed and long—in fact, a splendid baby. Everybody was exceedingly proud of him, especially his father and mother, the King and Queen of Nomansland, who had waited for him during their happy reign of ten years—now made happier than ever, to themselves and their subjects, by the appearance of a son and heir.

The only person who was not quite happy was the King's brother, the heir presumptive, who would have been king one day had the baby not been born. But as his Majesty was very kind to him, and even rather sorry for him—insomuch that at the Queen's request he gave him a dukedom almost as big as a county—the Crown Prince, as he was called, tried to seem pleased also; and let us hope he succeeded.

The Prince's christening was to be a grand affair. According to the custom of the country, there were chosen for him four-and-twenty godfathers and godmothers, who each had to give him a name, and promise to do their utmost for him. When he came of age, he himself had to choose the name—and the godfather or godmother—that he liked the best, for the rest of his days.

Meantime all was rejoicing. Subscriptions were made among the rich to give pleasure to the poor; dinners in town halls for the workingmen; tea parties in the streets for their wives; and milk-and-bun feasts for the children in the schoolrooms. For Nomansland, though I cannot point it out on any map or read of it in any history, was, I believe, much like our own or many another country.

As for the palace—which was no different from other palaces—it was clean "turned out of the windows," as people say, with the preparations going on. The only quiet place in it was the room which, though the Prince was six weeks old, his mother the Queen had never quitted. Nobody said she was ill, however —it would have been so inconvenient. And as she said nothing about it herself, but lay pale and placid, giving no trouble to anybody, nobody thought much about her. All the world was absorbed in admiring the baby.

The christening day came at last, and it was as lovely as the Prince himself. All the people in the palace were lovely too—or thought themselves so—in the elegant new clothes which the Queen, who thought of everybody, had taken care to give them, from the ladies-in-waiting down to the poor little kitchenmaid, who looked at herself in her pink cotton gown, and thought, doubtless, that there never was such a pretty girl as she.

By six in the morning all the royal household had dressed itself in its very best. And then the little Prince was dressed in his best—his magnificent christening robe; which proceeding his Royal Highness did not like at all, but kicked and screamed like any common baby. When he had calmed down a little, they carried him to be looked at by the Queen his mother, who, though her royal robes had been brought and laid upon the bed, was, as everybody well knew, quite unable to rise and put them on.

She admired her baby very much; kissed and blessed him, and lay looking at him, as she did for hours sometimes, when he was placed beside her fast asleep. Then she gave him up with a gentle smile, and, saying she hoped he would be very good, that it

would be a very nice christening, and all the guests would enjoy themselves, turned peacefully over on her bed, saying nothing more to anybody. She was a very uncomplaining person, the Queen—and her name was Dolorez.

Everything went on exactly as if she had been present. All, even the King himself, had grown used to her absence; for she was not strong, and for years had not joined in any gaieties. She always did her royal duties, but as to pleasures, they could go on quite well without her, or it seemed so. The company arrived: great and notable persons in this and neighboring countries; also the four-and-twenty godfathers and godmothers, who had been chosen with care, as the people who would be most useful to his Royal Highness should he ever want friends, which did not seem likely. What such want could possibly happen to the heir of the powerful monarch of Nomansland?

They came, walking two and two, with their coronets on their heads—being dukes and duchesses, princes and princesses, or the like. They all kissed the child and pronounced the name each had given him. Then the four-and-twenty names were shouted out with great energy by six heralds, one after the other, and afterward written down, to be preserved in the state records, in readiness for the next time they were wanted, which would be either on his Royal Highness's coronation or his funeral.

Soon the ceremony was over, and everybody satisfied; except, perhaps, the little Prince himself, who moaned faintly under his christening robes, which nearly smothered him.

In truth, though very few knew, the Prince in coming to the chapel had met with a slight disaster. His nurse—not his ordinary one, but the state nursemaid—an elegant and fashionable young lady of rank, whose duty it was to carry him to and from the chapel, had been so occupied in arranging her train with one hand, while she held the baby with the other, that she stumbled and let him fall, just at the foot of the marble staircase.

To be sure, she contrived to pick him up again the next minute; and the accident was so slight it seemed hardly worth speaking of. Consequently nobody did speak of it. The baby had turned deadly pale, but did not cry, so no person a step or two behind could discover anything wrong. Afterward, even if he had moaned, the silver trumpets were loud enough to drown his voice. It would have been a pity to let anything trouble such a day of felicity.

So, after a minute's pause, the procession had moved on. Such a procession! Heralds in blue and silver; pages in crimson and gold; and a troop of little girls in dazzling white, carrying baskets of flowers, which they strewed all the way before the nurse and child. Finally the four-and-twenty godfathers and godmothers, as proud as possible, and so splendid to look at that they would have quite extinguished their small godson—merely a heap of lace and muslin with a baby face inside—had it not been for a canopy of white satin and ostrich feathers which was held over him wherever he was carried.

Thus, with the sun shining on them through the

painted windows, they stood; the King and his train on one side, the Prince and his attendants on the other, as pretty a sight as ever was seen out of fairyland.

"It's just like fairyland," whispered the eldest little girl to the next eldest, as she shook the last rose out of her basket; "and I think the only thing the Prince wants now is a fairy godmother."

"Does he?" said a shrill but soft and not unpleasant voice behind; and there was seen among the group of children somebody—not a child, yet no bigger than a child—somebody whom nobody had seen before, and who certainly had not been invited, for she had no christening clothes on.

She was a little old woman dressed all in gray: gray gown; gray hooded cloak, of a material excessively fine, and a tint that seemed perpetually changing, like the gray of an evening sky. Her hair was gray, and her eyes also—even her complexion had a soft gray shadow over it. But there was nothing unpleasantly old about her, and her smile was as sweet and childlike as the Prince's own, which stole over his pale little face the instant she came near enough to touch him.

"Take care! Don't let the baby fall again."

The grand young lady nurse started, flushing angrily.

"Who spoke to me? How did anybody know?—I

mean, what business has anybody—" Then, frightened, but still speaking in a much sharper tone than I
hope young ladies of rank are in the habit of speaking—"Old woman, you will be kind enough not to
say 'the baby,' but 'the Prince.' Keep away; his Royal
Highness is just going to sleep."

"Nevertheless I must kiss him. I am his godmother."

"You!" cried the elegant lady nurse.

"You!" repeated all the gentlemen- and ladies-in-
waiting.

"You!!!" echoed the heralds and pages—and they
began to blow the silver trumpets in order to stop all
further conversation.

The Prince's procession formed itself for returning—the King and his train having already moved
off toward the palace—but on the topmost step of the
marble stairs stood, right in front of all, the little old
woman clothed in gray.

She stretched herself on tiptoe by the help of her
stick, and gave the little Prince three kisses.

"This is intolerable!" cried the young lady nurse,
wiping the kisses off rapidly with her lace handkerchief. "Such an insult to his Royal Highness! Take
yourself out of the way, old woman, or the King shall
be informed immediately."

"The King knows nothing of me, more's the pity,"
replied the old woman, with an indifferent air, as if

It was as pretty a sight as ever was seen out of fairyland

t she had done so, and it was very like her to do it
he had turned with her face to the window,
ence one could just see the tops of the distant
untains—the Beautiful Mountains, as they were
led—where she was born. So gazing, she had
ietly passed away.

When the little Prince was carried back to his
ther's room, there was no mother to kiss him. And,
ugh he did not know it, there would be for him no
ther's kiss any more.

As for his godmother—the little old woman in gray
o called herself so—whether she melted into air,
e her gown when they touched it, or whether she
w out the chapel window, or slipped through
e doorway among the bewildered crowd, nobody
ew—nobody ever thought about her.

Only the nurse, the ordinary homely one, coming
it of the Prince's nursery in the middle of the night
search of a cordial to quiet his continual moans,
w, sitting in the doorway, something which she
ould have thought a mere shadow had she not seen
ining out of it two eyes, gray and soft and sweet.
he put her hands before her own, screaming loudly.
Vhen she took them away the old woman was gone.

she thought the loss was more on his Majesty's side
than hers. "My friend in the palace is the King's
wife."

"Kings have not wives, but queens," said the lady
nurse, with a contemptuous air.

"You are right," replied the old woman. "Nevertheless, I know her Majesty well, and I love her and
her child. And—since you dropped him on the marble
stairs [this she said in a mysterious whisper, which
made the young lady tremble in spite of her anger]
—I choose to take him for my own, and be his godmother, ready to help him whenever he wants me."

"You help him!" cried all the group, breaking into
shouts of laughter, to which the little old woman paid
not the slightest attention. Her soft gray eyes were
fixed on the Prince, who seemed to answer to the
look, smiling again and again in the causeless, aimless
fashion that babies do smile.

"His Majesty must hear of this," said a gentleman-
in-waiting.

"His Majesty will hear quite enough news in a
minute or two," said the old woman sadly. And again
stretching up to the little Prince, she kissed him on
the forehead solemnly.

"Be called by a new name which nobody has ever
thought of. Be Prince Dolor, in memory of your
mother Dolorez."

"In memory of!" Everybody started at the ominous

14

their coronation day, and it nev
again till it was engraved on their
died.

"Old woman, you are exceeding
the eldest lady-in-waiting, much h
could know the fact passes my co
even if you did know it, how dare
hint that her most gracious Majes
rez?"

"*Was* called Dolorez," said the o
tender solemnity.

The first gentleman, called the g
ing, raised it to strike her, and all t
out their hands to seize her; but
melted from between their fingers l
fore anybody had time to do anyth
came a heavy, muffled, startling soun

The great bell of the palace—the
heard only on the death of someor
family, and for as many times as he
old—began to toll. They listened, m
stricken. Someone counted: one—tv
—up to nine-and-twenty—just the Que

It was, indeed, the Queen. Her Maj
In the midst of the festivities she ha
out of her new happiness and her old
few nor small. Sending away all her wc
grand sight—at least they said afterw

phrase, and also at a most terrible breach of etiquette
which the old woman had committed. In Nomansland, neither the King nor the Queen was supposed
to have any Christian name at all. They dropped it on

CHAPTER 2

EVERYBODY WAS VERY KIND to the poor little Prince. I think people generally are kind to motherless children, whether princes or peasants. He had a magnificent nursery and a regular suite of attendants, and was treated with the greatest respect and state. Nobody was allowed to talk to him in silly baby language, or dandle him, or above all to kiss him, though perhaps some people did it surreptitiously, for he was such a sweet baby that it was difficult to help it.

It could not be said that the Prince missed his mother—children of his age cannot do that; but somehow after she died everything seemed to go wrong with him. From a beautiful baby he became sickly and pale, seeming to have almost ceased growing, especially in his legs, which had been so fat and strong.

But after the day of his christening they withered and shrank. He no longer kicked them out in either passion or play, and when, as he got to be nearly a year old, his nurse tried to make him stand upon them, he only tumbled down.

This happened so many times that at last people began to talk about it. A prince, and not able to stand on his own legs! What a dreadful thing! What a misfortune for the country!

Rather a misfortune to him also, poor little boy! but nobody seemed to think of that. And when, after a while, his health revived, and the old bright look came back to his sweet little face, and his body grew larger and stronger, though still his legs remained the same, people continued to speak of him in whispers, and with grave shakes of the head. Everybody knew, though nobody said it, that something, it was impossible to guess what, was not quite right with the poor little Prince.

Of course, nobody hinted this to the King his father. It does not do to tell great people anything unpleasant. And besides, his Majesty took very little notice of his son, or of his other affairs, beyond the necessary duties of his kingdom.

People had said he would not miss the Queen at all, she having been so long an invalid, but he did. After her death he never was quite the same. He established himself in her empty rooms, the only rooms in the palace whence one could see the Beautiful Mountains, and was often observed looking at them as if he thought she had flown away thither, and that his longing could bring her back again. And by a curious coincidence, which nobody dared inquire into, he desired that the Prince might be called, not by any of the four-and-twenty grand names given him by his godfathers and godmothers, but by the identical name mentioned by the little old woman in gray—Dolor, after his mother Dolorez.

Once a week, according to established state custom, the Prince, dressed in his very best, was brought to the King his father for half an hour, but his Majesty was generally too ill and too melancholy to pay much heed to the child.

Only once, when he and the Crown Prince, who was exceedingly attentive to his royal brother, were sitting together, with Prince Dolor playing in a corner of the room, dragging himself about with his arms rather than his legs, and sometimes trying feebly to crawl from one chair to another, it seemed to strike the father that all was not right with his son.

"How old is his Royal Highness?" said he suddenly to the nurse.

"Two years, three months, and five days, please your Majesty."

"It does not please me," said the King, with a sigh. "He ought to be far more forward than he is now—ought he not, brother? You, who have so many children, must know. Is there not something wrong about him?"

"Oh, no," said the Crown Prince, exchanging meaning looks with the nurse, who did not understand at all, but stood frightened and trembling with the tears in her eyes. "Nothing to make your Majesty at all uneasy. No doubt his Royal Highness will outgrow it in time."

"Outgrow—what?"

"A slight delicacy—ahem!—in the spine; something inherited, perhaps, from his dear mother."

"Ah, she was always delicate; but she was the

sweetest woman that ever lived. Come here, my little son."

And as the Prince turned round upon his father a small, sweet, grave face—so like his mother's—his Majesty the King smiled and held out his arms. But when the boy came to him, not running like a boy, but wriggling awkwardly along the floor, the royal countenance clouded over.

"I ought to have been told of this. It is terrible—terrible! And for a prince too. Send for all the doctors in my kingdom immediately."

They came, and each gave a different opinion and ordered a different mode of treatment. The only thing they agreed in was what had been pretty well known before, that the Prince must have been hurt when he was an infant—let fall, perhaps, so as to injure his spine and lower limbs. Did nobody remember?

No, nobody. Indignantly, all the nurses denied that any such accident had happened, was possible to have happened, until the faithful country nurse recollected that it really had happened on the day of the christening. For which unluckily good memory all the others scolded her so severely that she had no peace of her life, and soon after, by the influence of the young lady nurse who had carried the baby that fatal day, and who was a sort of connection of the Crown Prince—being his wife's second cousin once removed—the poor woman was pensioned off and sent to the Beautiful Mountains from whence she came, with orders to remain there for the rest of her days.

But of all this the King knew nothing, for, indeed, after the first shock of finding out that his son could not walk, and seemed never likely to walk, he interfered very little concerning him. The whole thing was too painful, and his Majesty never liked painful things. Sometimes he inquired after Prince Dolor, and they told him his Royal Highness was going on as well as could be expected, which really was the case. For, after worrying the poor child and perplexing themselves with one remedy after another, the Crown Prince, not wishing to offend any of the differing doctors, had proposed leaving him to Nature; and Nature, the safest doctor of all, had come to his help and done her best.

He could not walk, it is true. His limbs were mere useless appendages to his body; but the body itself was strong and sound. And his face was the same as ever—just his mother's face, one of the sweetest in the world.

Even the King, indifferent as he was, sometimes looked at the little fellow with sad tenderness, noticing how cleverly he learned to crawl and swing himself about by his arms, so that in his own awkward way he was as active in motion as most children of his age.

"Poor little man! he does his best, and he is not unhappy—not half so unhappy as I, brother," addressing the Crown Prince, who was more constant than ever in his attendance upon the sick monarch. "If anything should befall me, I have appointed you Regent. In case of my death, you will take care of my poor little boy?"

"Certainly, certainly; but do not let us imagine any such misfortune. I assure your Majesty—everybody will assure you—that it is not in the least likely."

He knew, however, and everybody knew, that it was likely, and soon after it actually did happen. The King died as suddenly and quietly as the Queen had done—indeed, in her very room and bed; and Prince Dolor was left without either father or mother—as sad a thing as could happen, even to a prince.

He was more than that now, though. He was a king. In Nomansland, as in other countries, the people were struck with grief one day and revived the next. "The King is dead—long live the King!" was the cry that rang through the nation, and almost before his late Majesty had been laid beside the Queen in their splendid mausoleum, crowds came thronging from all parts to the royal palace, eager to see the new monarch.

They did see him—the Prince Regent took care
they should—sitting on the floor of the council chamber, sucking his thumb! And when one of the gentle-
men-in-waiting lifted him up and carried him—fancy
carrying a king!—to the chair of state, and put the
crown on his head, he shook it off again, it was so
heavy and uncomfortable. Sliding down to the foot
of the throne he began playing with the golden lions
that supported it, stroking their paws and putting his
tiny fingers into their eyes, and laughing—laughing
as if he had at last found something to amuse him.

"There's a fine king for you!" said the first lord-in-
waiting, a friend of the Prince Regent's (the Crown
Prince that used to be, who, in the deepest mourning,
stood silently beside the throne of his young nephew;
he was a handsome man, very grand and clever-
looking). "What a king! who can never stand to receive his subjects, never walk in processions, who to
the last day of his life will have to be carried about
like a baby. Very unfortunate!"

"Exceedingly unfortunate," repeated the second
lord. "It is always bad for a nation when its king is a
child; but such a child—a permanent cripple, if not
worse."

"Let us hope not worse," said the first lord in a very
hopeless tone, and looking toward the Regent, who
stood erect and pretended to hear nothing. "I have
heard that these children with very large heads, and

great broad foreheads and staring eyes, are—well, well, let us hope for the best and be prepared for the worst. In the meantime—"

"I swear," said the Crown Prince, coming forward and kissing the hilt of his sword—"I swear to perform my duties as Regent, to take all care of his Royal Highness—his Majesty, I mean," with a grand bow to the little child, who laughed innocently back again. "And I will do my humble best to govern the country. Still, if the country has the slightest objection—"

But the Crown Prince being generalissimo, having the whole army at his beck and call, so that he could have begun a civil war in no time, the country had, of course, not the slightest objection.

So the King and Queen slept in their tomb in peace, and Prince Dolor reigned over the land—that is, his uncle did; and everybody said what a fortunate thing it was for the poor little Prince to have such a clever uncle to take care of him.

All things went on as usual. Indeed, after the Regent had brought his wife and her seven sons, and established them in the palace, they went on rather better than usual. For they gave such splendid entertainments and made the capital so lively that trade revived, and the country was said to be more flourishing than it had been for a century.

Whenever the Regent and his sons appeared, they were received with shouts: "Long live the Crown Prince!" "Long live the royal family!" And, in truth, they were very fine children, the whole seven of them, and made a great show when they rode out together on seven beautiful horses, one height above another, down to the youngest, on his tiny black pony, no bigger than a large dog.

As for the other child, his Royal Highness Prince Dolor—for somehow people soon ceased to call him his Majesty, which seemed such a ridiculous title for a poor little fellow, a helpless cripple—with only head and trunk, and no legs to speak of—he was seen very seldom by anybody.

Sometimes people daring enough to peer over the high wall of the palace garden noticed there, carried in a footman's arms, or drawn in a chair, or left to play on the grass, often with nobody to mind him, a pretty little boy, with a bright, intelligent face and large, melancholy eyes—no, not exactly melancholy, for they were his mother's, and she was by no means sad-minded, but thoughtful and dreamy. They rather perplexed people, those childish eyes; they were so exceedingly innocent and yet so penetrating. If anybody did a wrong thing—told a lie, for instance—they would turn round with such a grave, silent surprise— the child never talked much—that every naughty person in the palace was rather afraid of Prince Dolor.

He could not help it, and perhaps he did not even know it, being no better a child than many other children, but there was something about him which made bad people sorry, and grumbling people ashamed of themselves, and ill-natured people gentle and kind.

I suppose because they were touched to see a poor little fellow who did not in the least know what had befallen him or what lay before him, living his baby life as happily as the day is long. Thus, whether or not he was good himself, the sight of him and his affliction made other people good, and, above all,

made everybody love him—so much so that his uncle
the Regent began to feel a little uncomfortable.

Now, I have nothing to say against uncles in general. They are usually very excellent people, and very
convenient to little boys and girls. Even the "cruel
uncle" of the *Babes in the Wood* I believe to be
quite an exceptional character. And this "cruel uncle"
of whom I am telling was, I hope, an exception, too.

He did not mean to be cruel. If anybody had called
him so, he would have resented it extremely. He

would have said that what he did was done entirely for the good of the country. But he was a man who had always been accustomed to consider himself first and foremost, believing that whatever he wanted was sure to be right, and therefore he ought to have it. So he tried to get it, and got it too, as people like him very often do. Whether they enjoy it when they have it is another question.

Therefore he went one day to the council chamber, determined on making a speech, and informing the ministers and the country at large that the young King was in failing health, and that it would be advisable to send him for a time to the Beautiful Mountains. Whether he really meant to do this, or whether it occurred to him afterward that there would be an easier way of attaining his great desire, the crown of Nomansland, is a point which I cannot decide.

But soon after, when he had obtained an order in council to send the King away—which was done in great state, with a guard of honor composed of two whole regiments of soldiers—the nation learned, without much surprise, that the poor little Prince— nobody ever called him king now—had gone on a much longer journey than to the Beautiful Mountains.

He had fallen ill on the road and died within a few hours; at least so declared the physician in attendance and the nurse who had been sent to take care of him. They brought his coffin back in great state, and buried it in the mausoleum with his parents.

So Prince Dolor was seen no more. The country went into deep mourning for him, and then forgot him, and his uncle reigned in his stead. That illustri-

ous personage accepted his crown with great decorum, and wore it with great dignity to the last. But
whether he enjoyed it or not there is no evidence to
show.

CHAPTER 3

AND WHAT of the little lame Prince, whom everybody seemed so easily to have forgotten?

Not everybody. There were a few kind souls, mothers of families, who had heard his sad story, and some servants about the palace, who had been familiar with his sweet ways—these many a time sighed and said, "Poor Prince Dolor!" Or, looking at the Beautiful Mountains, which were visible all over Nomansland, though few people ever visited them, "Well, perhaps his Royal Highness is better where he is than even there."

They did not know—indeed, hardly anybody did know—that beyond the mountains, between them and the sea, lay a tract of country, barren, level, bare, except for short, stunted grass, and here and there a patch of tiny flowers. Not a bush—not a tree—not a resting place for bird or beast was in that dreary plain. In summer the sunshine fell upon it hour after hour with a blinding glare. In winter the winds and rains swept over it unhindered, and the snow came down steadily, noiselessly, covering it from end to end in one great white sheet, which lay for days and weeks unmarked by a single footprint.

Not a pleasant place to live in—and nobody did live there, apparently. The only sign that human creatures had ever been near the spot was one large round tower which rose up in the center of the plain, and might be seen from every part of it—if there had been anybody to see, which there never was. Rose right up out of the ground, as if it had grown of itself, like a mushroom. But it was not at all mushroomlike; on the contrary, it was very solidly built. In form it resembled the Irish round towers, which have puzzled people for so long, nobody being able to find out when, or by whom, or for what purpose they were made; seemingly for no use at all, like this tower. It was circular, of very firm brickwork, with neither doors nor windows, until near the top, when you could perceive some slits in the wall through which one might possibly creep in or look out. Its height was nearly a hundred feet, and it had a battlemented parapet showing sharp against the sky.

As the plain was quite desolate—almost like a desert, only without sand, and led to nowhere except the still more desolate seacoast—nobody ever crossed it. Whatever mystery there was about the tower, it and the sky and the plain kept their secret to themselves.

It was a very great secret indeed—a state secret—which none but so clever a man as the present King of Nomansland would ever have thought of. How he carried it out, undiscovered, I cannot tell. People said, long afterward, that it was by means of a gang of condemned criminals, who were set to work, and executed immediately after they had finished, so that nobody knew anything, or in the least suspected the real fact.

And what was the fact? Why, that this tower, which seemed a mere mass of masonry, utterly forsaken and uninhabited, was not so at all. Within twenty feet of the top some ingenious architect had planned a perfect little house, divided into four rooms—as by drawing a cross within a circle you will see might easily be done. By making skylights, and a few slits in the walls for windows, and raising a peaked roof which was hidden by the parapet, here was a dwelling complete, eighty feet from the ground, and as inaccessible as a rook's nest on the top of a tree.

A charming place to live in! if you once got up there—and never wanted to come down again.

Inside—though nobody could have looked inside except a bird, and hardly even a bird flew past that lonely tower—inside it was furnished with all the comfort and elegance imaginable; with lots of books and toys, and everything that the heart of a child could desire. For its only inhabitant, except a nurse of course, was a poor solitary child.

One winter's night, when all the plain was white with moonlight, there was seen crossing it a great tall black horse, ridden by a man also big and equally black, carrying before him on the saddle a woman and a child. The woman—she had a sad, fierce look, and no wonder, for she was a criminal under sentence of death, but her sentence had been changed to almost as severe a punishment. She was to inhabit the lonely tower with the child, and was allowed to live as long as the child lived—no longer. This in order that she might take the utmost care of him; for those who put him there were equally afraid of his dying and of his living.

Yet he was only a little, gentle boy, with a sweet, sleepy smile—he had been very tired from his long journey—and with clinging arms, which held tight to the man's neck, for he was rather frightened, and the face, black as it was, looked kindly at him. And he was very helpless, with his poor, small, shriveled legs, which could neither stand nor run away—for the little forlorn boy was Prince Dolor.

He had not been dead at all—or buried either. His grand funeral had been a mere pretense: a wax figure having been put in his place, while he himself was spirited away under charge of these two, the condemned woman and the black man. The latter was deaf and dumb, so could neither tell nor repeat anything.

When they reached the foot of the tower, there was light enough to see a huge chain dangling from the parapet, but dangling only halfway. The deaf-mute took from his saddle wallet a sort of ladder, arranged in pieces like a puzzle, fitted it together, and lifted it up to meet the chain. Then he mounted to the top of the tower, and slung from it a sort of chair, in which the woman and the child placed themselves and were drawn up, never to come down again as long as they lived. Leaving them there, the man descended the ladder, took it to pieces again and packed it in his pack, mounted the horse and disappeared across the plain.

Every month they used to watch for him, appearing like a speck in the distance. He fastened his horse to the foot of the tower, and climbed it, as before, laden with provisions and many other things. He always saw the Prince, so as to make sure that the child was alive and well, and then went away until the following month.

While his first childhood lasted, Prince Dolor was

happy enough. He had every luxury that even a prince could need, and the one thing wanting—love —never having known, he did not miss. His nurse was very kind to him though she was a wicked woman. But either she had not been quite so wicked as people said, or she grew better through being shut up continually with a little innocent child who was dependent upon her for every comfort and pleasure of his life.

It was not an unhappy life. There was nobody to tease or ill-use him, and he was never ill. He played about from room to room—there were four rooms, parlor, kitchen, his nurse's bedroom, and his own; learned to crawl like a fly, and to jump like a frog, and to run about on all fours almost as fast as a puppy. In fact, he was very much like a puppy or a kitten, as thoughtless and as merry—scarcely ever cross, though sometimes a little weary.

As he grew older, he occasionally liked to be quiet for a while, and then he would sit at the slits of windows—which were, however, much bigger than they looked from the bottom of the tower—and watch the sky above and the ground below, with the storms sweeping over and the sunshine coming and going, and the shadows of the clouds running races across the blank plain.

By and by he began to learn lessons—not that his nurse had been ordered to teach him, but she did

The frightened little boy held tight to the man's neck

it partly to amuse herself. She was not a stupid woman, and Prince Dolor was by no means a stupid boy; so they got on very well, and his continual entreaty, "What can I do? what can you find me to do?" was stopped, at least for an hour or two in the day.

It was a dull life, but he had never known any other; anyhow, he remembered no other, and he did not pity himself at all. Not for a long time, till he grew quite a big little boy, and could read quite easily. Then he suddenly took to books, which the deaf-mute brought him from time to time—books which, not being acquainted with the literature of Nomansland, I cannot describe, but no doubt they were very interesting; and they informed him of everything in the outside world, and filled him with an intense longing to see it.

From this time a change came over the boy. He began to look sad and thin, and to shut himself up for hours without speaking. For his nurse hardly spoke, and whatever questions he asked beyond their ordinary daily life she never answered. She had, indeed, been forbidden, on pain of death, to tell him anything about himself, who he was, or what he might have been.

He knew he was Prince Dolor, because she always addressed him as "my Prince" and "your Royal Highness," but what a prince was he had not the least idea. He had no idea of anything in the world, except what he found in his books.

He sat one day surrounded by them, having built them up round him like a little castle wall. He had been reading them half the day, but feeling all the while that to read about things which you never can see is like hearing about a beautiful dinner while you are starving. For almost the first time in his life he grew melancholy; his hands fell on his lap; he sat gazing out the window slit upon the view outside —the view he had looked at every day of his life, and might look at for endless days more.

Not a very cheerful view—just the plain and the sky—but he liked it. He used to think, if he could only fly out that window, up to the sky or down to the plain, how nice it would be! Perhaps when he died—his nurse had told him once in anger that he would never leave the tower till he died—he might be able to do this. Not that he understood much what dying meant, but it must be a change, and any change seemed to him a blessing.

"And I wish I had somebody to tell me all about it—about that and many other things; somebody that would be fond of me, like my poor white kitten."

Here the tears came into his eyes, for the boy's one friend, the one interest of his life, had been a little white kitten, which the deaf-mute, kindly smiling, once took out of his pocket and gave him—the only living creature Prince Dolor had ever seen.

For four weeks it was his constant plaything and companion, till one moonlight night it took a fancy for wandering, climbed onto the parapet of the tower, dropped over and disappeared. It was not killed, he hoped, for cats have nine lives; indeed, he almost fancied he saw it pick itself up and scamper away; but he never caught sight of it again.

"Yes, I wish I had something better than a kitten —a person, a real live person, who would be fond of me and kind to me. Oh, I want somebody—dreadfully, dreadfully!"

As he spoke, there sounded behind him a slight tap-tap-tap, as of a stick or a cane, and twisting himself round, he saw—what do you think he saw?

Nothing either frightening or ugly, but still exceedingly curious. A little woman, no bigger than he might himself have been had his legs grown like those of other children; but she was not a child—she was an old woman. Her hair was gray, and her dress was gray, and there was a gray shadow over her wherever she moved. But she had the sweetest smile, the prettiest hands, and when she spoke it was in the softest voice imaginable.

"My dear little boy"—and dropping her cane, the only bright and rich thing about her, she laid those two tiny hands on his shoulders—"my own little boy, I could not come to you until you had said you wanted me; but now you do want me, here I am."

"And you are very welcome, madam," replied the Prince, trying to speak politely, as princes always did in books; "and I am exceedingly obliged to you. May I ask who you are? Perhaps my mother?" For he knew that little boys usually had a mother, and had occasionally wondered what had become of his own.

"No," said the visitor, with a tender, half-sad smile, putting back the hair from his forehead, and looking right into his eyes—"no, I am not your mother, though she was a dear friend of mine; and you are as like her as ever you can be."

"Will you tell her to come and see me, then?"

"She cannot; but I dare say she knows all about

you. And she loves you very much—and so do I; and I want to help you all I can, my poor little boy."

"Why do you call me poor?" asked Prince Dolor, in surprise.

The little old woman glanced down on his legs and feet, which he did not know were different from those of other children, and then at his sweet, bright face, which, though he knew not that either, was exceedingly different from many children's faces, which are often so fretful, cross, sullen. Looking at him, instead of sighing, she smiled. "I beg your pardon, my Prince," said she.

"Yes, I am a prince, and my name is Dolor; will you tell me yours, madam?"

The little old woman laughed like a chime of silver bells.

"I have not got a name—or, rather, I have so many names that I don't know which to choose. However, it was I who gave you yours, and you will belong to me all your days. I am your godmother."

"Hurrah!" cried the little Prince; "I am glad I belong to you, for I like you very much. Will you come and play with me?"

So they sat down together and played. By and by they began to talk.

"Are you very dull here?" asked the little old woman.

"Not particularly, thank you, godmother. I have plenty to eat and drink, and my lessons to do, and my books to read—lots of books."

"And you want nothing?"

"Nothing. Yes—perhaps— If you please, god-mother, could you bring me just one more thing?"

"What sort of thing?"

"A little boy to play with."

The old woman looked very sad. "Just the thing, alas! which I cannot give you. My child, I cannot alter your lot in any way, but I can help you to bear it."

"Thank you. But why do you talk of bearing it? I have nothing to bear."

"My poor little man!" said the old woman in the very tenderest tone of her tender voice. "Kiss me!"

"What is kissing?" asked the wondering child.

His godmother took him in her arms and embraced him many times. By and by he kissed her back again —at first awkwardly and shyly, then with all the strength of his warm little heart.

"You are better to cuddle than even my white kitten, I think. Promise me that you will never go away."

"I must; but I will leave a present behind me— something as good as myself to amuse you—some-thing that will take you wherever you want to go, and show you all that you wish to see."

"What is it?"

"A traveling cloak."

The Prince's countenance fell. "I don't want a cloak, for I never go out. Sometimes nurse hoists me onto the roof, and carries me round by the parapet; but that is all. I can't walk, you know, as she does."

"The more reason why you should ride; and besides, this traveling cloak—"

"Hush!—she's coming."

There sounded outside the room door a heavy step and a grumpy voice, and a rattle of plates and dishes.

"It's my nurse, and she is bringing my dinner; but I don't want dinner at all—I only want you. Will her coming drive you away, godmother?"

"Perhaps; but only for a little while. Never mind; all the bolts and bars in the world couldn't keep me out. I'd fly in at the window, or down through the chimney. Only wish for me, and I come."

"Thank you," said Prince Dolor, but almost in a whisper, for he was very uneasy at what might happen next. His nurse and his godmother—what would they say to one another? how would they look at one another?—two such different faces: one harsh-lined, sullen, cross, and sad; the other sweet and bright and calm as a summer evening before the dark begins.

When the door was flung open, Prince Dolor shut his eyes, trembling all over. Opening them again, he saw he need fear nothing—his lovely old godmother had melted away just like the rainbow out of the sky, as he had watched it many a time. Nobody but his nurse was in the room.

"What a muddle your Royal Highness is sitting in," said she sharply. "Such a heap of untidy books; and what's this rubbish?" knocking a little bundle that lay beside them.

"Oh, nothing, nothing—give it me!" cried the Prince, and, darting after it, he hid it under his pinafore, and then pushed it quickly into his pocket. Rubbish as it was, it was left in the place where she sat, and might be something belonging to her—his dear, kind godmother, whom already he loved with all his lonely, tender, passionate heart.

It was, though he did not know this, his wonderful traveling cloak.

CHAPTER 4

AND WHAT of the traveling cloak? What sort of cloak was it, and what good did it do the Prince?

Stay, and I'll tell you all about it.

Outside it was the commonest-looking bundle imaginable—shabby and small; and the instant Prince Dolor touched it, it grew smaller still, dwindling down till he could put it in his trousers pocket, like a handkerchief rolled up into a ball. He did this at once, for fear his nurse should see it, and kept it there all day—all night, too. Till after his next morning's lessons he had no opportunity of examining his treasure.

When he did, it seemed no treasure at all; but a mere piece of cloth—circular in form, dark green in

color—that is, if it had any color at all, being so worn
and shabby, though not dirty. It had a split cut to
the center, forming a round hole for the neck—and
that was all its shape; the shape, in fact, of those
cloaks which in South America are called ponchos
—very simple, but most graceful and convenient.

Prince Dolor had never seen anything like it. In
spite of his disappointment, he examined it curi-
ously. He spread it out on the floor, then arranged
it on his shoulders. It felt very warm and comfortable; but it was so exceedingly shabby—the only
shabby thing that the Prince had ever seen in his
life.

"And what use will it be to me?" said he sadly.
"I have no need of outdoor clothes, as I never go out.
Why was this given me? I wonder. And what in the
world am I to do with it? She must be a rather funny
person, this dear godmother of mine."

Nevertheless, because she was his godmother, and
had given him the cloak, he folded it carefully and
put it away, poor and shabby as it was, hiding it in
a safe corner of his top cupboard, which his nurse
never meddled with. He did not want her to find it,
or to laugh at it or at his godmother—as he felt sure
she would, if she knew all.

There it lay, and by and by he forgot all about it.
Nay, I am sorry to say that, being but a child, and
not seeing her again, he almost forgot his sweet old

godmother, or thought of her only as he did of the angels or fairies that he read of in his books, and of her visit as if it had been a mere dream of the night.

There were times, certainly, when he recalled her: of early mornings, like that morning when she appeared beside him, and late evenings, when the gray twilight reminded him of the color of her hair and her pretty soft garments; above all, when, waking in the middle of the night, with the stars peering in at his window, or the moonlight shining across his little bed, he would not have been surprised to see her standing beside it, looking at him with those beautiful tender eyes, which seemed to have a pleasantness and comfort in them different from anything he had ever known.

But she never came, and gradually she slipped out of his memory—only a boy's memory, after all; until something happened which made him remember her, and want her as he had never wanted anything before.

Prince Dolor fell ill. He caught—his nurse could not tell how—a complaint common to the people of Nomansland, called the doldrums, as unpleasant as measles or any other of our complaints; and it made him restless, cross, and disagreeable. Even when a little better, he was too weak to enjoy anything, but lay all day long on his sofa, fidgeting his nurse extremely—while, in her intense terror lest he might die, she fidgeted him still more. At last, seeing he really was getting well, she left him to himself—which he was most glad of, in spite of his dullness and dreariness. There he lay, alone, quite alone.

Now and then an irritable fit came over him, in which he longed to get up and do something, or to go somewhere. He would have liked to imitate his white kitten—jump down from the tower and run away, taking the chance of whatever might happen.

Only one thing, alas! was likely to happen; for the kitten, he remembered, had four active legs, while he—

"I wonder what my godmother meant when she looked at my legs and sighed so bitterly? I wonder why I can't walk straight and steady like my nurse —only I wouldn't like to have her great, noisy, clumping shoes. Still it would be very nice to move about quickly—perhaps to fly, like a bird, like that string of birds I saw the other day skimming across the sky, one after the other."

These were the passage birds—the only living creatures that ever crossed the lonely plain; and he had been much interested in them, wondering whence they came and whither they were going.

"How nice it must be to be a bird! If legs are no good, why cannot one have wings? People have wings when they die—perhaps. I wish I were dead, that I do. I am so tired, so tired; and nobody cares for me. Nobody ever did care for me, except perhaps my godmother. Godmother, dear, have you quite forsaken me?"

He stretched himself wearily, gathered himself up, and dropped his head upon his hands; as he did so, he felt somebody kiss him at the back of his neck, and, turning, found that he was resting, not on the sofa pillows, but on a warm shoulder—that of the little old woman clothed in gray.

How glad he was to see her! How he looked into her kind eyes and felt her hands, to see if she were all real and alive! Then he put both his arms round her neck, and kissed her as if he would never have done kissing.

"Stop, stop!" cried she, pretending to be smothered. "I see you have not forgotten my teachings. Kissing is a good thing—in moderation. Only just let me have breath to speak one word."

"A dozen!" he said.

"Well, then, tell me all that has happened to you since I saw you—or, rather, since you saw me, which is quite a different thing."

"Nothing has happened—nothing ever does happen to me," answered the Prince dolefully.

"And are you very dull, my boy?"

"So dull that I was just thinking whether I could not jump down to the bottom of the tower, like my white kitten."

"Don't do that, not being a white kitten."

"I wish I were—I wish I were anything but what I am."

"And you can't make yourself any different, nor can I do it either. You must be content to stay just what you are."

The little old woman said this—very firmly, but gently, too—with her arms round his neck and her lips on his forehead. It was the first time the boy had ever heard anyone talk like this, and he looked up in surprise—but not in pain, for her sweet manner softened the hardness of her words.

"Now, my Prince—for you are a prince, and must behave as such—let us see what we can do; how much I can do for you, or show you how to do for yourself. Where is your traveling cloak?"

Prince Dolor blushed extremely. "I—I put it away in the cupboard. I suppose it is there still."

"You have never used it; you dislike it?"

He hesitated, not wishing to be impolite. "Don't you think it's—just a little old and shabby for a prince?"

The old woman laughed—long and loud, though very sweetly.

"Prince, indeed! Why, if all the princes in the world craved for it, they couldn't get it, unless I gave it them. Old and shabby! It's the most valuable thing imaginable! Very few ever have it; but I thought I would give it to you, because—because you are different from other people."

"Am I?" said the Prince, and looked first with curiosity, then with a sort of anxiety, into his godmother's face, which was sad and grave, with slow tears beginning to steal down.

She touched his poor little legs. "These are not like those of other little boys."

"Indeed!—my nurse never told me that."

"Very likely not. But it is time you were told; and I tell you, because I love you."

"Tell me what, dear godmother?"

"That you will never be able to walk or run or jump or play—that your life will be quite different from most people's lives; but it may be a very happy life for all that. Do not be afraid."

"I am not afraid," said the boy. But he turned very pale, and his lips began to quiver, though he did not actually cry—he was too old for that, and, perhaps, too proud.

Though not wholly comprehending, he began dimly to guess what his godmother meant. He had never seen any real live boys, but he had seen pictures of them running and jumping; which he had admired and tried hard to imitate, but always failed. Now he began to understand why he failed, and that he always should fail—that, in fact, he was not like other little boys; and it was of no use his wishing to do as they did, and play as they played, even if he had had them to play with. His was a separate life, in which he must find out new work and new pleasures for himself.

The sense of *the inevitable,* as grown-up people call it—that we cannot have things as we want them to be, but as they are, and that we must learn to bear them and make the best of them—this lesson, which everybody has to learn soon or late—came, alas! sadly soon to the poor boy. He fought against it for a while, and then, quite overcome, turned and sobbed bitterly in his godmother's arms.

She comforted him—I do not know how, except that love always comforts. And then she whispered to him, in her sweet, strong, cheerful voice: "Never mind!"

"No, I don't think I do mind—that is, I *won't* mind," replied he, catching the courage of her tone and speaking like a man, though he was still such a mere boy.

"That is right, my Prince!—that is being like a prince. Now we know exactly where we are; let us put our shoulders to the wheel and—"

"We are in Hopeless Tower [this was its name, if it had a name], and there is no wheel to put our shoulders to," said the child sadly.

"You little matter-of-fact goose! Well for you that you have a godmother called—"

"What?" he eagerly asked.

"Stuff-and-nonsense."

"Stuff-and-nonsense! What a funny name!"

"Some people give it me, but they are not my most intimate friends. These call me—never mind what," added the old woman, with a soft twinkle in her eyes. "So as you know me, and know me well, you may give me any name you please; it doesn't matter. But I am your godmother, child. I have few godchildren. Those I have love me dearly, and find me the greatest blessing in all the world."

"I can well believe it," cried the little lame Prince, and forgot his troubles in looking at her—as her figure dilated, her eyes grew lustrous as stars, her very raiment brightened, and the whole room seemed filled with her beautiful and beneficent presence like light.

He could have looked at her forever—half in love, half in awe; but she suddenly dwindled down into the little old woman all in gray, and, with a malicious twinkle in her eyes, asked for the traveling cloak.

"Bring it out of the rubbish cupboard, and shake the dust off it, quick!" said she to Prince Dolor, who hung his head, rather ashamed. "Spread it out on the floor, and wait till the split closes and the edges turn up like a rim all round. Then go and open the skylight—mind, I say *open the skylight*—set yourself down in the middle of it, like a frog on a water-lily leaf; say 'Abracadabra, dum dum dum,' and—see what will happen!"

The Prince burst into a fit of laughing. It all seemed so exceedingly silly; he wondered that a wise old woman like his godmother should talk such nonsense.

"Stuff-and-nonsense, you mean," said she, answering, to his great alarm, his unspoken thoughts. "Did I not tell you some people called me by that name? Never mind; it doesn't harm me."

And she laughed—her merry laugh—as childlike as if she were the Prince's age instead of her own, whatever that might be. She certainly was a most extraordinary old woman.

"Believe me or not, it doesn't matter," said she. "Here is the cloak. When you want to go traveling on it, say 'Abracadabra, dum dum dum'; when you want to come back again, say 'Abracadabra, tum tum ti.' That's all; good-by."

A puff of most pleasant air passing by him, making him feel for the moment quite strong and well, was all the Prince was conscious of. His most extraordinary godmother was gone.

"Really now, how rosy your Royal Highness's cheeks have grown! You seem to have got well already," said the nurse, entering the room.

"I think I have," replied the Prince very gently—

he felt gentle and kind even to his grim nurse. "And now let me have my dinner, and go you to your sewing as usual."

The instant she was gone, however, taking with her the plates and dishes, which for the first time since his illness he had satisfactorily cleared, Prince Dolor hopped down from his sofa, and with one or two of his froglike jumps reached the cupboard where he kept his toys, and looked everywhere for his traveling cloak.

Alas! it was not there.

While he was ill of the doldrums, his nurse, thinking it a good opportunity for putting things to rights, had made a grand clearance of all his "rubbish"—as she considered it. His beloved headless horses, broken carts, sheep without feet, and birds without wings—all the treasures of his baby days, which he could not bear to part with, were gone. Though he seldom played with them now, he liked just to feel they were there.

They were all gone and with them the traveling cloak. He sat down on the floor, looking at the empty shelves, so beautifully clean and tidy, then burst out sobbing as if his heart would break.

But quietly—always quietly. He never let his nurse hear him cry. She only laughed at him, as he felt she would laugh now.

"And it is all my own fault!" he cried. "I ought to have taken better care of my godmother's gift. Oh, godmother, forgive me! I'll never be so careless again. I don't know what the cloak is exactly, but I am sure it is something precious. Help me to find it again. Oh, don't let it be stolen from me—don't, please!"

"Ha, ha, ha!" laughed a silvery voice. "Why, that traveling cloak is the one thing in the world which nobody can steal. It is of no use to anybody except the owner. Open your eyes, my Prince, and see what you shall see."

His dear old godmother, he thought, and turned eagerly round. But no; he beheld, lying in a corner of the room, all dust and cobwebs, his precious traveling cloak.

Prince Dolor darted toward it, tumbling several times on the way, as he often did tumble, poor boy!

and pick himself up again, never complaining. Snatching it to his breast, he hugged and kissed it, cobwebs and all, as if it had been something alive. Then he began unrolling it, wondering each minute what would happen. What did happen was so curious that I must leave it for another chapter.

CHAPTER 5

IF ANY READER, big or little, should wonder whether there is a meaning in this story deeper than that of an ordinary fairy tale, I will own that there is. But I have hidden it so carefully that the smaller people, and many larger folk, will never find it out, and meantime the book may be read straight on, like *Cinderella*, or *Bluebeard*, or *Hop-o'-My-Thumb*, for what interest it has or what amusement it may bring.

Having said this, I return to Prince Dolor, that little lame boy whom many may think so exceedingly to be pitied. But if you had seen him as he sat patiently untying his wonderful cloak, which was done up in a very tight and perplexing parcel, using skillfully his deft little hands, and knitting his brows with firm determination, while his eyes glistened with pleasure and energy and eager anticipation—if you had beheld him thus, you might have changed your opinion.

When we see people suffering or unfortunate, we feel very sorry for them. But when we see them bravely bearing their sufferings and making the best of their misfortunes, it is quite a different feeling. We respect, we admire them. One can respect and admire even a little child.

When Prince Dolor had patiently untied all the knots, a remarkable thing happened. The cloak began to undo itself. Slowly unfolding, it laid itself down on the carpet, as flat as if it had been ironed. The split joined with a little sharp crick-crack, and the rim turned up all round till it was breast-high. Meantime the cloak had grown and grown, and become quite large enough for one person to sit in it as comfortably as if in a boat.

The Prince watched it rather anxiously; it was such an extraordinary, not to say a frightening, thing. However, he was no coward, but a thorough boy, who, if he had been like other boys, would doubtless have grown up daring and adventurous— a soldier, a sailor, or the like. As it was, he could only show his courage morally, not physically, by being afraid of nothing, and by doing boldly all that it was in his narrow powers to do. And I am not sure but that in this way he showed more real valor than if he had had six pairs of proper legs.

He said to himself: "What a goose I am! As if my dear godmother would ever have given me anything to hurt me. Here goes!"

So, with one of his active leaps, he sprang right into the middle of the cloak, where he squatted down, wrapping his arms tight round his knees, for they shook a little and his heart beat fast. But there he sat, steady and silent, waiting for what might happen next.

Nothing did happen, and he began to think nothing would, and to feel rather disappointed, when he recollected the words he had been told to repeat—"Abracadabra, dum dum dum!"

He repeated them, laughing all the while, they seemed such nonsense. And then—and then—

Now I don't expect anybody to believe what I am going to relate, though a good many wise people have believed a good many sillier things. And as seeing's believing, and I never saw it, I cannot be expected implicitly to believe it myself, except in a sort of way. And yet there is truth in it—for some people.

The cloak rose, slowly and steadily, at first only a few inches, then gradually higher and higher, till it nearly touched the skylight. Prince Dolor's head actually bumped against the glass, or would have done so had he not crouched down, crying, "Oh, please don't hurt me!" in a most melancholy voice.

Then he suddenly remembered his godmother's express command—"Open the skylight!"

Regaining his courage at once, without a moment's delay he lifted up his head and began searching for the bolt—the cloak meanwhile remaining perfectly still, balanced in the air. But the minute the window was opened, out it sailed—right out into the clear, fresh air, with nothing between it and the cloudless blue.

Prince Dolor had never felt any such delicious sensation before. I can understand it. Cannot you? Did you never think, in watching the rooks going home singly or in pairs, soaring their way across the calm evening sky till they vanish like black dots in the misty gray, how pleasant it must feel to be up there, quite out of the noise and din of the world, able to hear and see everything down below, yet troubled by nothing and teased by no one—all alone, but perfectly content?

Something like this was the happiness of the little lame Prince when he got out of Hopeless Tower, and found himself for the first time in the pure open air, with the sky above him and the earth below.

True, there was nothing but earth and sky; no houses, no trees, no rivers, mountains, seas—not a beast on the ground or a bird in the air. But to him even the level plain looked beautiful. And then there was the glorious arch of the sky, with a little young moon sitting in the west like a baby queen. And the evening breeze was so sweet and fresh—it

kissed him like his godmother's kisses. And by and by a few stars came out—first two or three, and then quantities—quantities! so that when he began to count them he was utterly bewildered.

By this time, however, the cool breeze had become cold. The mist gathered; and as he had, as he said, no outdoor clothes, poor Prince Dolor was not very comfortable. The dews fell damp on his curls. He began to shiver.

"Perhaps I had better go home," thought he.

But how? For in his excitement the other words which his godmother had told him to use had slipped his memory. They were only a little different from the first, but in that slight difference all the importance lay. As he repeated his "Abracadabra," trying ever so many other syllables after it, the cloak only went faster and faster, skimming on through the dusky, empty air.

The poor little Prince began to feel frightened. What if his wonderful traveling cloak should keep on thus traveling, perhaps to the world's end, carrying with it a poor, tired, hungry boy, who, after all, was beginning to think there was something very pleasant in supper and bed!

"Dear godmother," he cried pitifully, "do help me! Tell me just this once and I'll never forget again."

Instantly the words came rushing into his head —"Abracadabra, tum tum ti!" Was that it? Ah! yes— for the cloak began to turn slowly. He repeated the charm again, more distinctly and firmly, when it gave a gentle dip, like a nod of satisfaction, and immediately started back, as fast as ever, in the direction of the tower.

He reached the skylight, which he found exactly

as he had left it, and slipped in, cloak and all, as easily as he had got out. He had scarcely reached the floor, and was still sitting in the middle of his traveling cloak—like a frog on a water-lily leaf, as his godmother had expressed it—when he heard his nurse's voice outside.

"Bless us! what has become of your Royal Highness all this time? To sit stupidly here at the window till it is quite dark, and leave the skylight open, too. Prince! what can you be thinking of? You are the silliest boy I ever knew."

"Am I?" said he absently, and never heeding her crossness; for his only anxiety was lest she might find out what he had been doing.

She would have been a very clever person to have done so. The instant Prince Dolor got off it, the cloak folded itself up into the tiniest possible parcel, tied all its own knots, and rolled itself of its own accord into the farthest and darkest corner of the room. If the nurse had seen it, which she didn't, she would have taken it for a mere bundle of rubbish not worth noticing.

Shutting the skylight with an angry bang, she brought in the supper and lit the candles with her usual unhappy expression of countenance. But Prince Dolor hardly saw it. He saw only, hid in the corner where nobody else would see it, his wonderful traveling cloak. And though his supper was not

particularly nice, he ate it heartily, scarcely hearing
a word of his nurse's grumbling, which tonight
seemed to have taken the place of her sullen silence.

"Poor woman!" he thought, when he paused a
minute to listen and look at her with those quiet,
happy eyes, so like his mother's. "Poor woman! she
hasn't got a traveling cloak!"

And when he was left alone at last, and crept into
his little bed, where he lay awake a good while,
watching what he called his "sky-garden," all
planted with stars, like flowers, his chief thought
was—"I must be up very early tomorrow morning,
and get my lessons done, and then I'll go traveling
all over the world on my beautiful cloak."

So next day he opened his eyes with the sun, and
went with a good heart to his lessons. They had
hitherto been the chief amusement of his dull life.
Now, I am afraid, he found them also a little dull.
But he tried to be good—I don't say Prince Dolor
always was good, but he generally tried to be—and
when his mind went wandering after the dark, dusty
corner where lay his precious treasure, he resolutely
called it back again.

"For," he said, "how ashamed my godmother
would be of me if I grew up a stupid boy!"

But the instant lessons were done, and he was
alone in the empty room, he crept across the floor,
undid the shabby little bundle, his fingers trembling

with eagerness, climbed on the chair, and thence to the table, so as to unbar the skylight—he forgot nothing now—said his magic charm, and was away out the window, as children say, "in a few minutes less than no time."

Nobody missed him. He was accustomed to sit so quietly always that his nurse, though only in the next room, perceived no difference. And besides, she might have gone in and out a dozen times, and it would have been just the same; she never could have found out his absence.

For what do you think the clever godmother did? She took a quantity of moonshine, or some equally convenient material, and made an image, which she set on the window sill reading, or by the table drawing, where it looked so like Prince Dolor that any common observer would never have guessed the deception. And even the boy would have been puzzled to know which was the image and which was himself.

And all this while the happy little fellow was away, floating in the air on his magic cloak, and seeing all sorts of wonderful things—or they seemed wonderful to him, who had hitherto seen nothing at all.

First, there were the flowers that grew on the plain, which, whenever the cloak came near enough, he strained his eyes to look at. They were very tiny,

but very beautiful—white saxifrage, and yellow
lotus, and ground thistles, purple and bright, with
many others the names of which I do not know. No
more did Prince Dolor, though he tried to find them
out by recalling any pictures he had seen of them.
But he was too far off; and though it was pleasant
enough to admire them as brilliant patches of color,
still he would have liked to examine them all. He
was, as a little girl I know once said of a playfellow,
"a very examining boy."

"I wonder," he thought, "whether I could see
better through a pair of glasses like those my nurse
reads with, and takes such care of. How I would take
care of them, too, if I only had a pair!"

Immediately he felt something queer and hard
fixing itself to the bridge of his nose. It was a pair
of the prettiest gold spectacles ever seen. Looking
downward, he found that, though ever so high
above the ground, he could see every minute blade
of grass, every tiny bud and flower—nay, even the
insects that walked over them.

"Thank you, thank you!" he cried, in a gush of
gratitude—to anybody or everybody, but especially
to his dear godmother, who he felt sure had given
him this new present. He amused himself with it for
ever so long, with his chin pressed on the rim of the
cloak, gazing down upon the grass, every square foot
of which was a mine of wonders.

Then, just to rest his eyes, he turned them up to the sky—the blue, bright, empty sky, which he had looked at so often and seen nothing.

Now surely there was something. A long, black, wavy line, moving on in the distance, not by chance, as the clouds move apparently, but deliberately, as if it were alive. He might have seen it before—he almost thought he had; but then he could not tell what it was. Looking at it through his spectacles, he discovered that it really was alive; being a long string of birds, flying one after the other, their wings moving steadily and their heads pointed in one direction, as steadily as if each were a little ship, guided invisibly by an unerring helm.

"They must be the passage birds flying seaward!" cried the boy, who had read a little about them, and had a great talent for putting two and two together and finding out all he could. "Oh, how I should like to see them quite close, and to know where they come from and whither they are going! How I wish I knew everything in all the world!"

A silly speech for even an "examining" little boy to make; because, as we grow older, the more we know the more we find out there is to know. And Prince Dolor blushed when he had said it, and hoped nobody had heard him.

Apparently somebody had, however. For the cloak gave a sudden bound forward, and presently he found himself high in the air, in the very middle of that band of aerial travelers, who had no magic cloak to travel on—nothing except their wings. Yet there they were, making their fearless way through the sky.

Prince Dolor looked at them as one after the other they glided past him; and they looked at him— those pretty swallows with their changing necks and bright eyes—as if wondering to meet in mid-air such an extraordinary sort of bird.

"Oh, I wish I were going with you, you lovely creatures! I'm getting so tired of this dull plain, and the dreary and lonely tower. I do so want to see the world! Pretty swallows, dear swallows! tell me what it looks like—the beautiful, wonderful world!"

But the swallows flew past him—steadily, slowly pursuing their course as if inside each little head had been a mariner's compass, to guide him safe over land and sea, direct to the place where he wished to go.

The boy looked after them with envy. For a long time he followed with his eyes the faint, wavy black line as it floated away, sometimes changing its curves a little, but never deviating from its settled course, till it vanished entirely out of sight.

Then he settled himself down in the center of the cloak, feeling quite sad and lonely.

"I think I'll go home," said he, and repeated his

"Abracadabra, tum tum ti!" with a rather heavy
heart. The more he had, the more he wanted. It is
not always one can have everything one wants—at
least, at the exact minute one craves for it; not even

though one is a prince, and has a powerful and
beneficent godmother.

He did not like to vex her by calling for her and
telling her how unhappy he was, in spite of all her
goodness. So he just kept his trouble to himself, went
back to his lonely tower, and spent three days in
silent melancholy, without even attempting another
journey on his traveling cloak.

CHAPTER 6

HE FOURTH DAY it happened that the deaf-mute paid his accustomed visit, after which Prince Dolor's spirits rose. They always did when he got the new books which, just to relieve his conscience, the King of Nomansland regularly sent to his nephew; with many new toys also, though the latter were disregarded now.

"Toys, indeed! when I'm a big boy," said the Prince, with disdain, and would scarcely condescend to mount a rocking horse which had come, somehow or other—I can't be expected to explain things very exactly—packed on the back of the other, the great black horse, which stood and fed contentedly at the bottom of the tower.

Prince Dolor leaned over and looked at it, and thought how grand it must be to get upon its back— this grand live steed—and ride away, like the pictures of knights.

"Suppose I were a knight," he said to himself; "then I should be obliged to ride out and see the world."

But he kept all these thoughts to himself, and just sat still, devouring his new books till he had come to the end of them all. It was a repast not unlike the Barmecide feast which you read of in the *Arabian Nights,* which consisted of very elegant but empty dishes, or that supper of Sancho Panza in *Don Quixote,* where, the minute the smoking dishes came on the table, the physician waved his hand and they were all taken away.

Thus almost all the ordinary delights of boy life had been taken away from, or rather never given to this poor little prince.

"I wonder," he would sometimes think—"I wonder what it feels like to be on the back of a horse, galloping away, or holding the reins in a carriage, and tearing across the country, or jumping a ditch, or running a race, such as I read of or see in pictures. What a lot of things there are that I should like to do! But first I should like to go and see the world. I'll try."

Apparently it was his godmother's plan always to let him try, and try hard, before he gained anything. This day the knots that tied up his traveling cloak were more than usually troublesome, and he was a full half hour before he got out into the open air, and found himself floating merrily over the top of the tower.

Hitherto, in all his journeys, he had never let himself go out of sight of home, for the dreary building, after all, was home—he remembered no other. But now he felt sick of the very look of his tower, with its round smooth walls and level battlements.

"Off we go!" cried he, when the cloak stirred itself with a slight, slow motion, as if awaiting his orders. "Anywhere—anywhere, so that I am away from here, and out into the world."

As he spoke, the cloak, as if seized suddenly with a new idea, bounded forward and went skimming through the air, faster than the very fastest railway train.

"Gee-up! gee-up!" cried Prince Dolor in great excitement. "This is as good as riding a race."

And he patted the cloak as if it had been a horse— that is, in the way he supposed horses ought to be patted—and tossed his head back to meet the fresh breeze, and pulled his coat collar up and his hat down as he felt the wind grow keener and colder —colder than anything he had ever known.

"What does it matter, though?" said he. "I'm a boy, and boys ought not to mind anything."

Still, for all his good will, by and by, he began to

shiver exceedingly. Also, he had come away without his dinner, and he grew frightfully hungry. And to add to everything, the sunshiny day changed into rain, and being high up, in the very midst of the clouds, he got soaked through and through in a very few minutes.

"Shall I turn back?" meditated he. "Suppose I say 'Abracadabra'?"

Here he stopped, for already the cloak gave an obedient lurch, as if it were expecting to be sent home immediately.

"No—I can't—I can't go back! I must go forward and see the world. But oh! if I had but the shabbiest old rug to shelter me from the rain, or the driest morsel of bread and cheese, just to keep me from starving! Still, I don't much mind. I'm a prince, and ought to be able to stand anything. Hold on, cloak, we'll make the best of it."

It was a most curious circumstance, but no sooner had he said this than he felt stealing over his knees something warm and soft; in fact, a most beautiful bearskin, which folded itself round him quite naturally, and cuddled him up as closely as if he had been the cub of the kind old mother bear that once owned it. Then feeling in his pocket, which suddenly stuck out in a marvelous way, he found, not exactly bread and cheese, nor even sandwiches, but a packet of the most delicious food he had ever tasted. It was not meat, nor pudding, but a combination of both, and it served him excellently for both. He ate his dinner with the greatest gusto imaginable, till he grew so thirsty he did not know what to do.

"Couldn't I have just one drop of water, if it didn't trouble you too much, kindest of godmothers?"

For he really thought this want was beyond her power to supply. All the water which supplied Hopeless Tower was pumped up with difficulty from a deep artesian well—there were such things known in Nomansland—which had been drilled at the foot of it. But around, for miles upon miles, the desolate plain was perfectly dry. And above it, high in the air, how could he expect to find a well, or to get even a drop of water?

He forgot one thing—the rain. While he spoke, it came on in another wild burst, as if the clouds had poured themselves out in a passion of crying, wetting him certainly, but leaving behind, in a large glass vessel which he had never noticed before, enough water to quench the thirst of two or three boys at least. And it was so fresh, so pure—as water from the clouds always is when it does not catch the soot from city chimneys and other defilements—that he drank it, every drop, with the greatest delight and content.

Also, as soon as it was empty the rain filled it again, so that he was able to wash his face and hands and refresh himself exceedingly. Then the sun came out and dried him in no time. After that he curled himself up under the bearskin rug, and though he determined to be the most wide-awake boy imaginable, being so snug and warm and comfortable, Prince Dolor condescended to shut his eyes just for one minute. The next minute he was sound asleep.

When he awoke, he found himself floating over a country quite unlike anything he had ever seen before.

Yet it was nothing but what most of you children see every day and never notice it—a pretty country landscape, like England, Scotland, America, or any other land you choose to name. It had no particular features—nothing in it was grand or lovely. It was simply pretty, nothing more. Yet to Prince Dolor, who had never gone beyond his lonely tower and level plain, it appeared the most charming sight imaginable.

First, there was a river. It came tumbling down the hillside, frothing and foaming, playing at hide-and-seek among the rocks, then bursting out in noisy fun like a child, to bury itself in deep, still pools. Afterward it went steadily on for a while, like a good grown-up person, till it came to another big rock, where it misbehaved itself extremely. It turned into a cataract, and went tumbling over and over, after a fashion that made the Prince—who had never seen water before, except in his bath or his drinking cup —clap his hands with delight.

"It is so active, so alive! I like things active and alive!" cried he, and watched it shimmering and dancing, whirling and leaping, till, after a few windings and vagaries, it settled into a respectable stream. After that it went along, deep and quiet, but flowing steadily on, till it reached a large lake, into which it slipped and so ended its course.

All this the boy saw, either with his own naked

eyes or through his gold spectacles. He saw also as in a picture, beautiful but silent, many other things which struck him with wonder, especially a grove of trees.

Only think, to have lived to his age (which he himself did not know, as he did not know his own birthday) and never to have seen trees! As he floated over these oaks, they seemed to him—trunk, branches, and leaves—the most curious sight imaginable.

"If I could only get nearer, so as to touch them," said he, and immediately the obedient cloak ducked down. Prince Dolor made a snatch at the topmost twig of the tallest tree, and caught a bunch of leaves in his hand.

Just a bunch of green leaves—such as we see in myriads; watching them bud, grow, fall, and then kicking them along on the ground as if they were worth nothing. Yet how wonderful they are—every one of them a little different. I don't suppose you could ever find two leaves exactly alike in form, color, and size—no more than you could find two faces alike, or two characters exactly the same. The plan of this world is infinite similarity and yet infinite variety.

Prince Dolor examined his leaves with the greatest curiosity—and also a little caterpillar that he found walking over one of them. He coaxed it to

take an additional walk over his finger, which it did
with the greatest dignity and decorum, as if it, Mr.
Caterpillar, were the most important individual in
existence. It amused him for a long time; and when
a sudden gust of wind blew it overboard, leaves and
all, he felt quite disconsolate.

"Still there must be many live creatures in the
world besides caterpillars. I should like to see a few
of them."

The cloak gave a little dip down, as if to say "All right, my Prince," and bore him across the oak forest to a long fertile valley—called in Scotland a strath and in England a weald, but what they call it in the tongue of Nomansland I do not know. It was made up of cornfields, pasturefields, lanes, hedges, brooks, and ponds. Also, in it were what the Prince desired to see—a quantity of living creatures, wild and tame. Cows and horses, lambs and sheep, fed in the meadows; pigs and fowls walked about the farm-yards; and in lonelier places hares scudded, rabbits burrowed, and pheasants and partridges, with many other smaller birds, inhabited the fields and woods.

Through his wonderful spectacles the Prince could see everything. But, as I said, it was a silent picture; he was too high up to catch anything except a faint murmur, which only aroused his anxiety to hear more.

"I have as good as two pairs of eyes," he thought. "I wonder if my godmother would give me a second pair of ears."

Scarcely had he spoken than he found lying on his lap the most curious little parcel, all done up in silvery paper. And it contained—what do you think? Actually a pair of silver ears, which, when he tried them on, fitted so exactly over his own that he hardly felt them, except for the difference they made in his hearing.

There is something which we listen to daily and never notice. I mean the sounds of the visible world, animate and inanimate. Winds blowing, waters flowing, trees stirring, insects whirring (dear me! I am quite unconsciously writing rhyme), with the various cries of birds and beasts—lowing cattle, bleating sheep, grunting pigs, and cackling hens— all the infinite discords that somehow or other make a beautiful harmony.

We hear this, and are so accustomed to it that we think nothing of it. But Prince Dolor, who had lived all his days in the dead silence of Hopeless Tower, heard it for the first time. And oh! if you had seen his face.

He listened, listened, as if he could never have done listening. And he looked and looked, as if he could not gaze enough. Above all, the motion of the animals delighted him: cows walking, horses galloping, little lambs and calves running races across the meadows, were such a treat for him to watch—he that was always so quiet. But, these creatures having four legs, and he only two, the difference did not strike him painfully.

Still, by and by, after the fashion of children— and, I fear, of many big people too—he began to want something more than he had, something fresh and new.

"Godmother," he said, having now begun to believe that, whether he saw her or not, he could always speak to her with full confidence that she would hear him—"godmother, all these creatures I like exceedingly; but I should like better to see a creature like myself. Couldn't you show me just one little boy?"

There was a sigh behind him—it might have been only the wind—and the cloak remained so long balanced motionless in air that he was half afraid his godmother had forgotten him, or was offended with him for asking too much. Suddenly a shrill whistle startled him, even through his silver ears, and looking downward, he saw start up from behind a bush on a common, something—

Neither a sheep nor a horse nor a cow—nothing upon four legs. This creature had only two; but they were long, straight, and strong. And it had a lithe, active body, and a curly head of black hair set upon its shoulders. It was a boy, a shepherd boy, about the Prince's own age—but, oh! so different.

Not that he was an ugly boy—though his face was almost as red as his hands, and his shaggy hair matted like the backs of his own sheep. He was rather a nice-looking lad; and seemed so bright and healthy and good-tempered—"jolly" would be the word, only I am not sure if they have such a one in the elegant language of Nomansland—that the little Prince watched him with great admiration.

"Might he come and play with me? I would drop down to the ground to him, or fetch him up to me here. Oh, how nice it would be if I only had a little boy to play with me."

But the cloak, usually so obedient to his wishes, disobeyed him now. There were evidently some things which his godmother either could not or would not give. The cloak hung stationary, high in air, never attempting to descend. The shepherd lad evidently took it for a large bird, and, shading his eyes, looked up at it, making the Prince's heart beat fast.

However, nothing ensued. The boy turned round, with a long, loud whistle—seemingly his usual and only way of expressing his feelings. He could not make the thing out exactly—it was a rather mysterious affair, but it did not trouble him much—he was not an "examining" boy.

Then, stretching himself, for he had been evidently half asleep, he began flopping his shoulders with his arms to wake and warm himself; while his dog, a rough collie, who had been guarding the sheep meanwhile, began to jump upon him, barking with delight.

"Down, Snap, down! Stop that, or I'll thrash you," the Prince heard him say; though with such a rough, hard voice and queer pronunciation that it was difficult to make the words out. "Hollo! Let's warm ourselves by a race."

They started off together, boy and dog—barking and shouting, till it was doubtful which made the more noise or ran the faster. A regular steeplechase it was: first across the level common, greatly disturbing the quiet sheep; and then tearing away across country, scrambling through hedges and leaping ditches, and tumbling up and down over plowed fields. They did not seem to have anything to run for—but they ran as if they did it, both of them, for the mere pleasure of motion.

And what a pleasure that seemed! To the dog of course, but scarcely less so to the boy. How he skimmed along over the ground—his cheeks glowing, and his hair flying, and his legs—oh, what a pair of legs he had!

Prince Dolor watched him with great intentness, and in a state of excitement almost equal to that of the runner himself—for a while. Then the sweet, pale face grew a trifle paler, the lips began to quiver, and the eyes to fill.

"How nice it must be to run like that!" he said

softly, thinking that never—no, never in this world— would he be able to do the same.

Now he understood what his godmother had meant when she gave him his traveling cloak, and why he had heard that sigh—he was sure it was hers —when he had asked to see "just one little boy."

"I think I had rather not look at him again," said the poor little Prince, drawing himself back into the

center of his cloak, and resuming his favorite pos-
ture, sitting like a Turk, with his arms wrapped
round his feeble, useless legs.

"You're no good to me," he said, patting them
mournfully. "You never will be any good to me. I
wonder why I had you at all. I wonder why I was
born at all, since I was not to grow up like other
boys. Why not?"

A question so strange, so sad, yet so often occur-
ring in some form or other in this world—as you will
find, my children, when you are older—that even if
he had put it to his mother she could only have
answered it, as we have to answer many as difficult
things, by simply saying, "I don't know." There is
much that we do not know and cannot understand—
we big folks any more than you little ones. We have
to accept it all just as you have to accept anything
which your parents may tell you, even though you
don't as yet see the reason of it. You may sometime,
if you do exactly as they tell you, and are content to
wait.

Prince Dolor sat a good while thus, or it appeared
to him a good while, so many thoughts came and
went through his poor young mind—thoughts of
great bitterness, which, little though he was, seemed
to make him grow years older in a few minutes.

Then he fancied the cloak began to rock gently to
and fro, with a soothing kind of motion, as if he were

in somebody's arms, somebody who did not speak, but loved him and comforted him without need of words. Not by deceiving him with false encouragement or hope, but by making him see the plain, hard truth in all its hardness, and thus letting him quietly face it, till it became softened, and did not seem nearly so dreadful after all.

Through the dreary silence and blankness, for he had placed himself so that he could see nothing but the sky, and had taken off his silver ears as well as his gold spectacles—what was the use of either when he had no legs with which to walk or run?—up from below there rose a delicious sound.

You have heard it hundreds of times, my children, and so have I. When I was a child I thought there was nothing so sweet; and I think so still. It was just the song of a skylark, mounting higher and higher from the ground, till it came so close that Prince Dolor could distinguish its quivering wings and tiny body, almost too tiny to contain such a gush of music.

"Oh, you beautiful, beautiful bird!" cried he; "I should dearly like to take you in and cuddle you. That is, if I could—if I dared."

But he hesitated. The little brown creature with its loud heavenly voice almost made him afraid. Nevertheless, it also made him happy. And he watched and listened—so absorbed that he forgot all regret and pain, forgot everything in the world except the little lark.

It soared and soared, and he was just wondering if it would soar out of sight, and what in the world he should do when it was gone, when it suddenly closed its wings, as larks do when they mean to drop to the ground. But, instead of dropping to the ground, it dropped right into the little boy's breast.

What felicity! If it would only stay! A tiny, soft thing to fondle and kiss, to sing to him all day long, and be his playfellow and companion, tame and tender, while to the rest of the world it was a wild bird of the air. What a pride, what a delight! To have something that nobody else had—something all his own. As the traveling cloak traveled on, he little heeded where, and the lark still stayed, nestled down in his bosom, hopped from his hand to his shoulder, and kissed him with its dainty beak, as if it loved him. Prince Dolor forgot all his grief, and was entirely happy.

But when he got in sight of Hopeless Tower a painful thought struck him.

"My pretty bird, what am I to do with you? If I take you into my room and shut you up there, you, a wild skylark of the air, what will become of you? I am used to this, but you are not. You will be so miserable. And suppose my nurse should find you— she who can't bear the sound of singing? Besides, I remember her once telling me that the nicest thing she ever ate in her life was lark pie!"

The little boy shivered all over at the thought.

And, though the merry lark immediately broke into the loudest carol, as if saying derisively that he defied anybody to eat him, still Prince Dolor was very uneasy. In another minute he had made up his mind.

"No, my bird, nothing so dreadful shall happen to you if I can help it. I would rather do without you altogether. Yes, I'll try. Fly away, my darling, my beautiful! Good-by, my merry, merry bird."

Opening his two caressing hands, in which, as if for protection, he had folded it, he let the lark go. It lingered a minute, perching on the rim of the cloak, and looking at him with eyes of almost human tenderness. Then away it flew, far up into the blue sky. It was only a bird.

But some time afterward, when Prince Dolor had eaten his supper—somewhat drearily, except for the thought that he could not possibly sup off lark pie now—and gone quietly to bed, the old familiar little bed, where he was accustomed to sleep, or lie awake contentedly thinking—suddenly he heard outside the window a little faint carol—faint but cheerful— cheerful even though it was the middle of the night.

The dear little lark! it had not flown away, after all. And it was truly the most extraordinary bird, for, unlike ordinary larks, it kept hovering about the tower in the silence and darkness of the night, out- side the window or over the roof. Whenever he listened for a moment, he heard it singing still.

He went to sleep as happy as a king.

CHAPTER 7

"HAPPY AS A KING." How far kings are happy I cannot say, no more than could Prince Dolor, though he had once been a king himself. But he remembered nothing about it, and there was nobody to tell him, except his nurse, who had been forbidden upon pain of death to let him know anything about his dead parents, or the King his uncle, or indeed any part of his own history.

Sometimes he speculated about himself, whether he had had a father and mother as other little boys had, what they had been like, and why he had never seen them. But, knowing nothing about them, he did not miss them—only once or twice, reading pretty stories about little children and their mothers, who helped them when they were in difficulty and comforted them when they were sick, he, feeling ill and dull and lonely, wondered what had become of his mother and why she never came to see him.

Then, in his history lessons, of course, he read about kings and princes, and the governments of different countries, and the events that happened there. And though he but faintly took in all this, still he did take it in a little, and worried his young brain about it, and perplexed his nurse with questions, to which she returned sharp and mysterious answers, which only set him thinking the more.

He had plenty of time for thinking. After his last journey in the traveling cloak, the journey which had given him so much pain, his desire to see the world somehow faded away. He contented himself with reading his books, and looking out the tower windows, and listening to his beloved little lark, which had come home with him that day, and had never left him again.

True, it kept out of the way; and though his nurse sometimes dimly heard it, and said, "What is that horrid noise outside?" she never got the faintest chance of making it into a lark pie. Prince Dolor had his pet all to himself, and though he seldom saw it, he knew it was near him, and he caught continually, at odd hours of the day, and even in the night, fragments of its delicious song.

All during the winter—so far as there ever was any difference between summer and winter in Hopeless Tower—the little bird cheered and amused him. He scarcely needed anything more—not even his traveling cloak, which lay bundled up unnoticed in a corner, tied up in its innumerable knots.

Nor did his godmother come near him. It seemed as if she had given these treasures and left him alone —to use them or lose them, apply them or misapply them, according to his own choice. That is all we can do with children when they grow into big children old enough to distinguish between right and wrong, and too old to be forced to do either.

Prince Dolor was now quite a big boy. Not tall— alas! he never could be that, with his poor little shrunken legs, which were of no use, only an encumbrance. But he was stout and strong, with great sturdy shoulders, and muscular arms, upon which he could swing himself about almost like a monkey. As if in compensation for his useless lower limbs, Nature had given to these extra strength and activity. His face, too, was very handsome. It was thinner, firmer, more manly; but still the sweet face of his childhood—his mother's own face.

How his mother would have liked to look at him! Perhaps she did—who knows?

The boy was not a stupid boy either. He could learn almost anything he chose—and he did choose, which was more than half the battle. He never gave up his lessons till he had learned them all—never thought it a punishment that he had to work at them, and that they cost him a deal of trouble sometimes.

"But," thought he, "men work, and it must be so grand to be a man—a prince too; and I fancy princes work harder than anybody—except kings. The princes I read about generally turn into kings. I wonder—" the boy was always wondering. "Nurse" —and one day he startled her with a sudden question —"tell me—shall I ever be a king?"

The woman stood, perplexed beyond expression. So long a time had passed by since her crime—if it were a crime—and her sentence that she now seldom thought of either. Even her punishment—to be shut up for life in Hopeless Tower—she had gradually got used to. Used also to the little lame Prince, her charge—whom at first she had hated, though she carefully did everything to keep him alive, since upon him her own life hung.

But latterly she had ceased to hate him, and, in a sort of way, almost loved him—at least, enough to be sorry for him—an innocent child, imprisoned here till he grew into an old man, and became a dull, worn-out creature like herself. Sometimes, watching him, she felt more sorry for him than even for herself; and then, seeing she looked a less miserable and ugly woman, he did not shrink from her as usual.

He did not now. "Nurse—dear nurse," said he, "I don't mean to vex you, but tell me—what is a king? Shall I ever be one?"

When she began to think less of herself and more of the child, the woman's courage increased. The idea came to her—what harm would it be, even if he did know his own history? Perhaps he ought to know it—for there had been various ups and downs, usurpations, revolutions, and restorations in Nomansland, as in most other countries. Something might happen—who could tell? Changes might occur. Possibly a crown would even yet be set upon those pretty, fair curls—which she began to think prettier than ever when she saw the imaginary coronet upon them.

She sat down, considering whether her oath, never to "say a word" to Prince Dolor about himself, would be broken if she were to take a pencil and write what was to be told. A mere quibble—a mean, miserable quibble. But then she was a miserable woman, more to be pitied than scorned.

After long doubt, and with great trepidation, she put her fingers to her lips, and taking the Prince's slate—with the sponge tied to it, ready to rub out the writing in a minute—she wrote:

"You are a king."

Prince Dolor started. His face grew pale, and then flushed all over; he held himself erect. Lame as he was, anybody could see he was born to be a king.

"Hush!" said the nurse, as he was beginning to speak. And then, terribly frightened all the while— people who have done wrong always are frightened —she wrote down in a few hurried sentences his history. How his parents had died—his uncle had usurped his throne, and sent him to end his days in this lonely tower.

"I, too," added she, bursting into tears. "Unless, indeed, you could get out into the world, and fight for your rights like a man. And fight for me also, my Prince, that I may not die in this desolate place."

"Poor old nurse!" said the boy compassionately. For somehow, boy as he was, when he heard he was born to be a king, he felt like a man—like a king—who could afford to be tender because he was strong.

He scarcely slept that night, and even though he heard his little lark singing in the sunrise, he barely listened to it. Things more serious and important had taken possession of his mind.

"Suppose," thought he, "I were to do as she says, and go out in the world, no matter how it hurts me—the world of people, active people, as active as that boy I saw. They might only laugh at me—poor helpless creature that I am. But still I might show them I could do something. At any rate, I might go and see if there were anything for me to do. Godmother, help me!"

It was so long since he had asked her help that he was hardly surprised when he got no answer—only the little lark outside the window sang louder and louder, and the sun rose, flooding the room with light.

Prince Dolor sprang out of bed, and began dressing himself, which was hard work, for he was not used to it—he had always been accustomed to depend upon his nurse for everything.

"But I must now learn to be independent,"

thought he. "Fancy a king being dressed like a baby!"

So he did the best he could—awkwardly but cheerily—and then he leaped to the corner where lay his traveling cloak, untied it as before, and watched it unrolling itself—which it did rapidly, with a hearty good will, as if quite tired of idleness. So was Prince Dolor—or felt as if he were. He jumped into the middle of it, said his charm, and was out through the skylight immediately.

"Good-by, pretty lark!" he shouted, as he passed it on the wing, still warbling its carol to the newly risen sun. "You have been my pleasure, my delight; now I must go and work. Sing to old nurse till I come back again. Perhaps she'll hear you—perhaps she won't—but it will do her good all the same. Good-by!"

But, as the cloak hung irresolute in air, he suddenly remembered that he had not determined where to go—indeed, he did not know, and there was nobody to tell him.

"Godmother," he cried, in much perplexity, "you know what I want—at least, I hope you do, for I hardly do myself—take me where I ought to go. Show me whatever I ought to see—never mind what I like to see," as a sudden idea came into his mind that he might see many painful and disagreeable things. But this journey was not for pleasure—as be-

fore. He was not a baby now, to do nothing but play
—big boys do not always play. Nor men neither—
they work. Thus much Prince Dolor knew—though
very little more.

As the cloak started off, traveling faster than he
had ever known it to do—through sky-land and
cloud-land, over freezing mountaintops, and desolate stretches of forest, and smiling cultivated plains,
and great lakes that seemed to him almost as shore-
less as the sea—he was often rather frightened. But
he crouched down, silent and quiet; what was the
use of making a fuss? And, wrapping himself up in
his bearskin, he waited for what was to happen.

After some time he heard a murmur in the distance, increasing more and more till it grew like the
hum of a gigantic hive of bees. And, stretching his
chin over the rim of his cloak, Prince Dolor saw—
far, far below him, yet, with his gold spectacles and
silver ears on, he could distinctly hear and see—
what?

Most of us have some time or other visited a great
metropolis—have wandered through its network of
streets—lost ourselves in its crowds of people—looked
up at its tall rows of houses, its grand public build-
ings, churches, and squares. Also, perhaps, we have
peeped into its miserable little back alleys, where
dirty children play in gutters all day and half the
night—even young boys go about picking pockets,

with nobody to tell them it is wrong except the po-
liceman, and he simply takes them off to prison. And
all this wretchedness is close behind the grandeur—
like the two sides of the leaf of a book.

An awful sight is a large city, seen anyhow from
anywhere. But, suppose you were to see it from the
upper air, where, with your eyes and ears open, you
could take in everything at once? What would it
look like? How would you feel about it? I hardly
know myself. Do you?

Prince Dolor had need to be a king—that is, a boy
with a kingly nature—to be able to stand such a sight
without being utterly overcome. But he was very
much bewildered—as bewildered as a blind person
who is suddenly made to see.

He gazed down on the city below him, and then
put his hand over his eyes.

"I can't bear to look at it, it is so beautiful—so
dreadful. And I don't understand it—not one bit.
There is nobody to tell me about it. I wish I had
somebody to speak to."

"Do you? Then pray speak to me. I was always
considered good at conversation."

The voice that squeaked out this reply was an excellent imitation of the human one, though it came
only from a bird. No lark this time, however, but a
great black and white creature that flew into the
cloak, and began walking round and round on the

edge of it with a dignified stride, one foot before the other, like any unfeathered biped you could name.

"I haven't the honor of your acquaintance, sir," said the boy politely.

"Ma'am, if you please. I am a mother bird, and my name is Mag, and I shall be happy to tell you everything you want to know. For I know a great deal; and I enjoy talking. My family is of great antiquity. We have built in this palace for hundreds—that is to say, dozens of years. I am intimately acquainted with the King, the Queen, and the little Princes and Princesses—also the maids of honor, and all the inhabitants of the city. I talk a good deal, but I always talk sense, and I dare say I should be exceedingly useful to a poor little ignorant boy like you."

"I am a prince," said the other gently.

"All right. And I am a magpie. You will find me a most respectable bird."

"I have no doubt of it," was the polite answer— though he thought in his own mind that Mag must have a very good opinion of herself. But she was a lady and a stranger, so of course he was civil to her.

She settled herself at his elbow, and began to chatter away, pointing out with one skinny claw, while she balanced herself on the other, every object of interest, evidently believing, as no doubt all its inhabitants did, that there was no capital in the world like the great metropolis of Nomansland.

I have not seen it, and therefore cannot describe it, so we will just take it upon trust, and suppose it to be, like every other fine city, the finest city that ever was built. Mag said so—and of course she knew.

Nevertheless, there were a few things in it which surprised Prince Dolor—and, as he had said, he could not understand them at all. One half the people seemed so happy and busy—hurrying up and down the full streets, or driving lazily along the parks in their grand carriages, while the other half were so wretched and miserable.

"Can't the world be made a little more equal? I would try to do it if I were a king."

"But you're not the King: only a little goose of a boy," returned the magpie loftily. "And I'm here not to explain things, only to show them. Shall I show you the royal palace?"

It was a very magnificent palace. It had terraces and gardens, battlements and towers. It extended over acres of ground, and had in it rooms enough to accommodate half the city. Its windows looked in all directions, but none of them had any particular view —except a small one, high up toward the roof, which looked out on the Beautiful Mountains. But since the Queen died there it had been closed, boarded up, indeed, the magpie said. It was so little and inconvenient that nobody cared to live in it. Besides, the lower apartments, which had no view, were magnificent—worthy of being inhabited by the King.

"I should like to see the King," said Prince Dolor.

CHAPTER 8

WHAT, I WONDER, would be most people's idea of a king? What was Prince Dolor's?

Perhaps a very splendid personage, with a crown on his head and a scepter in his hand, sitting on a throne and judging the people. Always doing right, and never wrong—"The king can do no wrong" was a law laid down in olden times. Never cross, or tired, or sick, or suffering; perfectly handsome and well dressed, calm and good-tempered, ready to see and hear everybody, and discourteous to nobody; all things always going well with him, and nothing unpleasant ever happening.

This, probably, was what Prince Dolor expected

to see. And what did he see? But I must tell you how
he saw it.

"Ah," said the magpie, "no levee today. The King
is ill, though his Majesty does not wish it to be generally known—it would be so very inconvenient. He
can't see you, but perhaps you might like to go and
take a look at him in a way I often do? It is so very
amusing."

Amusing, indeed!

The Prince was just now too much excited to talk
much. Was he not going to see the King his uncle,
who had succeeded his father and dethroned himself; had stepped into all the pleasant things that he,
Prince Dolor, ought to have had, and shut him up in
a desolate tower? What was he like, this great, bad,
clever man? Had he got all the things he wanted,
which another ought to have had? And did he enjoy them?

"Nobody knows," answered the magpie, just as if
she had been sitting inside the Prince's heart, instead
of on the top of his shoulder. "He is a king, and that's
enough. For the rest nobody knows."

As she spoke, Mag flew down onto the palace
roof, where the cloak had rested, settling down between the great stacks of chimneys as comfortably
as if on the ground. She pecked at the tiles with her
beak—truly she was a wonderful bird—and immedi-

ately a little hole opened, a sort of door, through which could be seen distinctly the chamber below.

"Now look in, my Prince. Make haste, for I must soon shut it up again."

But the boy hesitated. "Isn't it rude?—won't they think us intruding?"

"Oh, dear, no! There's a hole like this in every palace; dozens of holes, indeed. Everybody knows it, but nobody speaks of it. Intrusion! Why, though the royal family are supposed to live shut up behind stone walls ever so thick, all the world knows that they live in a glass house where everybody can see them and throw a stone at them. Now pop down on your knees, and take a peep at his Majesty!"

His Majesty!

The Prince gazed eagerly down into a large room, the largest room he had ever beheld, with furniture and hangings grander than anything he could have ever imagined. A stray sunbeam, coming through a crevice of the darkened windows, struck across the carpet, and it was the loveliest carpet ever woven— just like a bed of flowers to walk over; only nobody walked over it, the room being perfectly empty and silent.

"Where is the King?" asked the puzzled boy.

"There," said Mag, pointing with one wrinkled claw to a magnificent bed, large enough to contain six people. In the center of it, just visible under the

The Prince gazed eagerly down into a large room

silken counterpane—quite straight and still—with its head on the lace pillow, lay a small figure, something like waxwork, fast asleep—very fast asleep! There were a number of sparkling rings on the tiny yellow hands, that were curled a little, helplessly, like a baby's, outside the coverlet. The eyes were shut, the nose looked sharp and thin, and the long gray beard hid the mouth and lay over the breast. A sight not ugly nor frightening, only solemn and quiet. And so very silent—two little flies buzzing about the curtains of the bed being the only audible sound.

"Is that the King?" whispered Prince Dolor.

"Yes," replied the bird.

He had been angry—furiously angry—ever since he knew how his uncle had taken the crown, and sent him, a poor little helpless child, to be shut up for life, just as if he had been dead. Many times the boy had felt as if, king as he was, he should like to strike him, this great, strong, wicked man.

Why, you might as well have struck a baby! How helpless he lay, with his eyes shut, and his idle hands folded. They had no more work to do, bad or good.

"What is the matter with him?" asked the Prince.

"He is dead," said the magpie, with a croak.

No, there was not the least use in being angry with him now. On the contrary, the Prince felt almost sorry for him, except that he looked so peaceful with all his cares at rest. And this was being dead? So even kings died?

"Well, well, he hadn't an easy life, folk say, for all his grandeur. Perhaps he is glad it is over. Good-by, your Majesty."

With another cheerful tap of her beak, Mistress Mag shut down the little door in the tiles, and Prince Dolor's first and last sight of his uncle was ended.

He sat in the center of his traveling cloak, silent and thoughtful.

"What shall we do now?" said the magpie. "There's nothing much more to be done with his Majesty, except a fine funeral, which I shall certainly go and see. All the world will. He interested the world exceedingly when he was alive, and he ought to do it now he's dead—just once more. And since he can't hear me, I may as well say that, on the whole, his Majesty is much better dead than alive—if we can only get somebody in his place. There'll be such a row in the city presently. Suppose we float up again and see it all—at a safe distance, though. It will be such fun!"

"What will be fun?"

"A revolution."

Whether anybody except a magpie would have called it "fun" I don't know, but it certainly was a remarkable scene.

As soon as the cathedral bell began to toll and

the minute guns to fire, announcing to the kingdom that it was without a king, the people gathered in crowds, stopping at street corners to talk together. The murmur now and then rose into a shout, and the shout into a roar. When Prince Dolor, quietly floating in upper air, caught the sound of their different and opposite cries, it seemed to him as if the whole city had gone mad together.

"Long live the King!" "The King is dead—down with the King!" "Down with the crown, and the King too!" "Hurrah for the republic!" "Hurrah for no government at all!"

Such were the shouts which traveled up to the traveling cloak. And then began—oh, what a scene!

When you children are grown men and women—or before—you will hear and read in books about what are called revolutions—earnestly I trust that neither I nor you may ever see one. But they have happened, and may happen again, in other countries besides Nomansland, when wicked kings have helped to make their people wicked too, or out of an unrighteous nation have sprung rulers equally bad; or, without either of these causes, when a restless country has fancied any change better than no change at all.

For me, I don't like changes, unless I am pretty sure that they are for good. And how good can come out of absolute evil—the horrible evil that went on this night under Prince Dolor's very eyes—soldiers shooting down people by hundreds in the streets, scaffolds erected, and heads dropping off—houses burned, and women and children murdered—this is more than I can understand.

But all these things you will find in history, my children, and must by and by judge for yourselves the right and wrong of them, as far as anybody ever can judge.

Prince Dolor saw it all. Things happened so fast one after another that they quite confused his faculties.

"Oh, let me go home," he cried at last, stopping his ears and shutting his eyes; "only let me go home!" For even his lonely tower seemed home, and its dreariness and silence absolute paradise after all this.

"Good-by, then," said the magpie, flapping her wings. She had been chatting incessantly all day and all night, for it was actually thus long that Prince Dolor had been hovering over the city, neither eating nor sleeping, with all these terrible things happening under his very eyes. "You've had enough, I suppose, of seeing the world?"

"Oh, I have—I have!" cried the Prince, with a shudder.

"That is, till next time. All right, your Royal Highness. You don't know me, but I know you. We may meet again sometime."

She looked at him with her clear, piercing eyes, sharp enough to see through everything, and it seemed as if they changed from bird's eyes to human eyes—the very eyes of his godmother, whom he had not seen for ever so long. But the minute afterward she became only a bird, and with a screech and a chatter, spread her wings and flew away.

Prince Dolor fell into a kind of swoon of utter misery, bewilderment, and exhaustion, and when he awoke he found himself in his own room—alone and quiet—with the dawn just breaking, and the long rim of yellow light in the horizon glimmering through the windowpanes.

CHAPTER 9

WHEN PRINCE DOLOR SAT UP in bed, trying to remember where he was, whither he had been, and what he had seen the day before, he perceived that his room was empty.

Generally his nurse rather worried him by breaking his slumbers, coming in and "setting things to rights," as she called it. Now the dust lay thick upon chairs and tables. There was no harsh voice heard to scold him for not getting up immediately, which, I am sorry to say, this boy did not always do. For he so enjoyed lying still, and thinking lazily about everything or nothing, that, if he had not tried hard to avoid it, he would certainly have become like those celebrated

Two little men
Who lay in their bed till the clock struck ten.

It was striking ten now, and still no nurse was to be seen. He was rather relieved at first, for he felt so tired. And besides, when he stretched out his arm, he found to his dismay that he had gone to bed in his clothes.

Very uncomfortable he felt, of course; and just a little frightened. Especially when he began to call and call again, but nobody answered. Often he used to think how nice it would be to get rid of his nurse and live in this tower all by himself—like a sort of monarch, able to do everything he liked, and leave undone all that he did not want to do. But now that this seemed really to have happened, he did not like it at all.

"Nurse—dear nurse—please come back!" he called out. "Come back, and I will be the best boy in all the land."

And when she did not come back, and nothing but silence answered his lamentable call, he very nearly began to cry.

"This won't do," he said at last, dashing the tears from his eyes. "It's just like a baby, and I'm a big boy —shall be a man someday. What has happened? I wonder. I'll go and see."

He sprang out of bed—not to his feet, alas! but to

his poor little weak knees, and crawled on them from room to room. All the four chambers were deserted —not forlorn or untidy, for everything seemed to have been done for his comfort—the breakfast and dinner things were laid, the food spread in order. He might live "like a prince," as the proverb is, for several days. But the place was entirely forsaken—there was evidently not a creature but himself in the solitary tower.

A great fear came over the poor boy. Lonely as his life had been, he had never known what it was to be absolutely alone. A kind of despair seized him—no violent anger or terror, but a sort of patient desolation.

"What in the world am I to do?" thought he, and sat down in the middle of the floor, half inclined to believe that it would be better to give up entirely, lay himself down, and die.

This feeling, however, did not last long, for he was young and strong, and, I said before, by nature a very courageous boy. There came into his head, somehow or other, a proverb that his nurse had taught him—the people of Nomansland were very fond of proverbs—

> For every evil under the sun
> There is a remedy, or there's none;
> If there is one, try to find it—
> If there isn't, never mind it.

"I wonder is there a remedy now, and could I find it?" cried the Prince, jumping up and looking out the window.

No help there. He saw only the broad, bleak, sun-shiny plain—that is, at first. But by and by, in the circle of mud that surrounded the base of the tower, he perceived distinctly the marks of a horse's feet, and just in the spot where the deaf-mute was ac-customed to tie up his great black charger, while he himself ascended, there lay the remains of a bundle of hay and a feed of corn.

"Yes, that's it. He has come and gone, taking nurse away with him. Poor nurse! how glad she would be to go!"

That was Prince Dolor's first thought. His second —wasn't it natural?—was a passionate indignation at her cruelty—at the cruelty of all the world to-ward him, a poor little helpless boy. Then he de-termined, forsaken as he was, to try and hold on to the last, and not to die as long as he could possibly help it.

Anyhow, it would be easier to die here than out in the world, among the terrible doings which he had just beheld—from the midst of which, it sud-denly struck him, the deaf-mute had come, contriv-ing somehow to make the nurse understand that the King was dead, and she need have no fear in going back to the capital, where there was a grand revolution, and everything turned upside down. So, of course, she had gone.

"I hope she'll enjoy it, miserable woman—if they don't cut off her head, too."

And then a kind of remorse smote him for feeling so bitterly toward her, after all the years she had taken care of him—grudgingly, perhaps, and coldly; still she had taken care of him, and that even to the last. For, as I have said, all his four rooms were as tidy as possible, and his meals laid out, that he might have no more trouble than could be helped.

"Possibly she did not mean to be cruel. I won't judge her," said he. And afterward he was very glad that he had so determined.

For the second time he tried to dress himself, and then to do everything he could for himself—even to sweeping up the hearth and putting on more coals. "It's a funny thing for a prince to have to do," said he, laughing. "But my godmother once said princes need never mind doing anything."

And then he thought a little of his godmother. Not of summoning her, or asking her to help him—she had evidently left him to help himself, and he was determined to try his best to do it, being a very proud and independent boy—but he remembered her tenderly and regretfully, as if even she had been a little hard upon him—poor, forlorn boy that he was.

But he seemed to have seen and learned so much within the last few days that he scarcely felt like a boy, but a man—until he went to bed at night.

When I was a child, I used often to think how nice it would be to live in a little house all by my own self—a house built high up in a tree, or far away in a forest, or halfway up a hillside—so deliciously alone and independent. Not a lesson to learn—but no! I always liked learning my lessons. Anyhow, to choose the lessons I liked best, to have as many books to read and dolls to play with as ever I wanted: above all, to be free and at rest, with nobody to tease or trouble or scold me, would be charming. For I was a lonely little thing, who liked quietness—as many children do; which other children, and sometimes grown-up people even, cannot understand. And so I can understand Prince Dolor.

After his first despair, he was not merely comfortable, but actually happy in his solitude, doing everything for himself, and enjoying everything by himself—until bedtime. Then he did not like it at all. No more, I suppose, than other children would have liked my imaginary house in a tree when they had had sufficient of their own company.

But the Prince had to bear it—and he did bear it, like a prince—for fully five days. All that time he got up in the morning and went to bed at night without having spoken to a creature, or, indeed, having heard a single sound. For even his little lark was silent. And as for his traveling cloak, either he never thought about it, or else it had been spirited away— for he made no use of it, nor attempted to do so.

A very strange existence it was, those five lonely days. He never entirely forgot it. It threw him back upon himself, and into himself—in a way that all of us have to learn when we grow up, and are the better for it; but it is somewhat hard learning.

On the sixth day Prince Dolor had a strange composure in his look, but he was very grave and thin and white. He had nearly come to the end of his provisions—and what was to happen next? Get out of the tower he could not. The ladder the deaf-mute used was always carried away again; and if it had not been, how could the poor boy have used it? And even if he slung or flung himself down, and by miraculous chance came alive to the foot of the tower, how could he run away?

Fate had been very hard on him, or so it seemed.

He made up his mind to die. Not that he wished to die. On the contrary, there was a great deal that he wished to live to do; but if he must die, he must. Dying did not seem so very dreadful; not even to lie quiet like his uncle, whom he had entirely forgiven now, and never be miserable or naughty any more, and escape all those horrible things that he had seen going on outside the palace, in that awful place which was called "the world."

"It's a great deal nicer here," said the poor little Prince, and collected all his pretty things round him: his favorite pictures, which he thought he should like to have near him when he died; his books and toys —no, he had ceased to care for toys now; he only liked them because he had done so as a child. And there he sat very calm and patient, like a king in his castle, waiting for the end.

"Still, I wish I had done something first—something worth doing, that somebody might remember me by," thought he. "Suppose I had grown a man, and had had work to do, and people to care for, and was so useful and busy that they liked me, and perhaps even forgot I was lame? Then it would have been nice to live, I think."

A tear came into the little fellow's eyes, and he listened intently through the dead silence for some hopeful sound.

Was there one?—was it his little lark, whom he had almost forgotten? No, nothing half so sweet. But it really was something—something which came nearer and nearer, so that there was no mistaking it. It was the sound of a trumpet, one of the great silver trumpets so admired in Nomansland. Not pleasant music, but very bold, grand, and inspiring.

As he listened to it the boy seemed to recall many

things which had slipped his memory for years, and to nerve himself for whatever might be going to happen.

What had happened was this.

The poor condemned woman had not been such a wicked woman after all. Perhaps her courage was not wholly disinterested, but she had done a very heroic thing. As soon as she heard of the death and burial of the King and of the changes that were taking place in the country, a daring idea came into her head—to set upon the throne of Nomansland its rightful heir. Thereupon she persuaded the deaf-mute to take her away with him, and they galloped like the wind from city to city, spreading everywhere the news that Prince Dolor's death and burial had been an invention concocted by his wicked uncle—that he was alive and well, and the noblest young Prince that ever was born.

It was a bold stroke, but it succeeded. The country, weary perhaps of the late King's harsh rule, and yet glad to save itself from the horrors of the last few days, and the still further horrors of no rule at all, and having no particular interest in the other young Princes, jumped at the idea of this Prince, who was the son of their late good King and the beloved Queen Dolorez.

"Hurrah for Prince Dolor! Let Prince Dolor be our sovereign!" rang from end to end of the kingdom. Everybody tried to remember what a dear baby he once was—how like his mother, who had been so sweet and kind, and his father, the finest-looking king that ever reigned. Nobody remembered his lameness—or, if they did, they passed it over as a matter of no consequence. They were determined to have him reign over them, boy as he was—perhaps just because he was a boy, since in that case the great nobles thought they should be able to do as they liked with the country.

Accordingly, with a fickleness not confined to the people of Nomansland, no sooner was the late King laid in his grave than they pronounced him to have been a usurper; turned all his family out of the palace, and left it empty for the reception of the new sovereign, whom they went to fetch with great rejoicing, a select body of lords, gentlemen, and soldiers traveling night and day in solemn procession through the country until they reached Hopeless Tower.

There they found the Prince, sitting calmly on the floor—deadly pale, indeed, for he expected a quite different end from this, and was resolved, if he had to die, to die courageously, like a prince and a king.

But when they hailed him as Prince and King, and explained to him how matters stood, and went down on their knees before him, offering the crown (on a velvet cushion, with four golden tassels, each nearly as big as his head)—small though he was and lame, which lameness the courtiers pretended not to notice—there came such a glow into his face, such a dignity into his demeanor, that he became beautiful, kinglike.

"Yes," he said, "if you desire it, I will be your king.

And I will do my best to make my people happy."

Then there arose, from inside and outside the tower, such a shout as never yet was heard across the lonely plain.

Prince Dolor shrank a little from the deafening sound. "How shall I be able to rule all this great people? You forget, my lords, that I am only a little boy still."

"Not so very little," was the respectful answer. "We have searched in the records, and found that your Royal Highness—your Majesty, I mean—is fifteen years old."

"Am I?" said Prince Dolor; and his first thought was a thoroughly childish pleasure that he should now have a birthday, with a whole nation to keep it. Then he remembered that his childish days were done. He was a monarch now. Even his nurse, to whom, the moment he saw her, he had held out his hand, kissed it reverently, and called him ceremoniously "his Majesty the King."

"A king must be always a king, I suppose," said he half sadly, when, the ceremonies over, he had been left to himself for just ten minutes, to put off his boy's clothes and be reattired in magnificent robes, before he was conveyed away from his tower to the royal palace.

He could take nothing with him; indeed, he soon saw that, however politely they spoke, they would

not allow him to take anything. If he was to be their
king, he must give up his old life forever. So he
looked with tender farewell on his old books, old
toys, the furniture he knew so well, and the familiar
plain in all its levelness—ugly yet pleasant, simply
because it was familiar.

"It will be a new life in a new world," said he to
himself; "but I'll remember the old things still. And,
oh! if before I go I could but once see my dear old
godmother."

While he spoke he had laid himself down on the
bed for a minute or two, rather tired with his grandeur, and confused by the noise of the trumpets
which kept playing incessantly down below. He
gazed, half sadly, up to the skylight, whence there
came pouring a stream of sun rays, with innumerable
motes floating there, like a bridge thrown between
heaven and earth. Sliding down it, as if she had been
made of air, came the little old woman in gray.

So beautiful looked she—old as she was—that
Prince Dolor was at first quite startled by the appari-
tion. Then he held out his arms in eager delight.

"Oh, godmother, you have not forsaken me!"

"Not at all, my son. You may not have seen me,
but I have seen you many a time."

"How?"

"Oh, never mind. I can turn into anything I please,

you know. And I have been a bearskin rug, and a crystal goblet—and sometimes I have changed from inanimate to animate nature, put on feathers, and made myself very comfortable as a bird."

"Ha!" laughed the Prince, a new light breaking in upon him as he caught the infection of her tone, lively and mischievous. "Ha! ha! a lark, for instance?"

"Or a magpie," answered she, with a capital imitation of Mistress Mag's croaky voice. "Do you suppose I am always sentimental, and never funny? If anything makes you happy, gay, or grave, don't you think it is more than likely to come through your old godmother?"

"I believe that," said the boy tenderly, holding out his arms. They clasped one another in a close embrace.

Suddenly Prince Dolor looked very anxious. "You will not leave me now that I am a king? Otherwise I had rather not be a king at all. Promise never to forsake me!"

The little old woman laughed gaily. "Forsake you? that is impossible. But it is just possible you may forsake me. Not probable though. Your mother never did, and she was a queen. The sweetest queen in all the world was the Lady Dolorez."

"Tell me about her," said the boy eagerly. "As I get older I think I can understand more. Do tell me."

"Not now. You couldn't hear me for the trumpets and the shouting. But when you are come to the palace, ask for a long-closed upper room, which looks out upon the Beautiful Mountains. Open it and take it for your own. Whenever you go there you will always find me, and we will talk together about all sorts of things."

"And about my mother?"

The little old woman nodded—and kept nodding and smiling to herself many times, as the boy repeated over and over again the sweet words he had never known or understood—"my mother—my mother."

"Now I must go," said she, as the trumpets blared louder and louder, and the shouts of the people showed that they would not endure any delay. "Good-by, good-by! Open the window and out I fly."

Prince Dolor repeated gaily the musical rhyme—but all the while tried to hold his godmother fast.

Vain, vain! for the moment that a knocking was heard at his door the sun went behind a cloud, the bright stream of dancing motes vanished, and the little old woman with them—he knew not where.

So Prince Dolor quitted his tower—which he had entered so mournfully and ignominiously as a little helpless baby carried in the deaf-mute's arms—quitted it as the great King of Nomansland.

The only thing he took away with him was something so insignificant that none of the lords, gentlemen, and soldiers who escorted him with such triumphant splendor could possibly notice it—a tiny bundle, which he had found lying on the floor just where the bridge of sunbeams had rested. At once he had pounced upon it, and thrust it secretly into his bosom, where it dwindled into such small proportions that it might have been taken for a mere chest comforter, a bit of flannel, or an old pocket handkerchief.

It was his traveling cloak!

CHAPTER 10

ID PRINCE DOLOR BECOME a great king? Was he, though little more than a boy, "the father of his people," as all kings ought to be? Did his reign last long—long and happy? And what were the principal events of it, as chronicled in the history of Nomansland?

Why, if I were to answer all these questions I should have to write another book. And I'm tired, children; tired—as grown-up people sometimes are, though not always with play. (Besides, I have a small person belonging to me, who, though she likes extremely to listen to the word-of-mouth story of this book, grumbles much at the writing of it, and has run about the house clapping her hands with joy when mamma told her that it was nearly finished. But that is neither here nor there.)

I have related as well as I could the history of Prince Dolor, but with the history of Nomansland I am as yet unacquainted. If anybody knows it, perhaps he or she will kindly write it all down in another book. But mine is done.

However, of this I am sure, that Prince Dolor made an excellent king. Nobody ever does anything less well, not even the commonest duty of common daily life, for having such a godmother as the little old woman clothed in gray, whose name is—well, I leave you to guess. Nor, I think, is anybody less good, less capable of both work and enjoyment in afterlife, for having been a little unhappy in his youth, as the Prince had been.

I cannot take upon myself to say that he was always happy now—who is?—or that he had no cares; just show me the person who is quite free from them! But whenever people worried and bothered him—as they did sometimes, with state etiquette, state squabbles, and the like, setting up themselves and pulling down their neighbors—he would take refuge in that upper room which looked out on the Beautiful Mountains, and, laying his head on his godmother's shoulder, become calmed and at rest.

Also, she helped him out of any difficulty which now and then occurred—for there never was such a wise old woman. When the people of Nomansland raised the alarm—as sometimes they did—for what people can exist without a little fault-finding?—and began to cry out, "Unhappy is the nation whose king is a child," she would say to him gently, "You are a child. Accept the fact. Be humble—be teachable. Lean upon the wisdom of others till you have gained your own."

He did so. He learned how to take advice before attempting to give it, to obey before he could righteously command. He assembled round him all the good and wise of his kingdom—laid all its affairs before them, and was guided by their opinions until he had maturely formed his own.

This he did sooner than anybody would have imagined who did not know of his godmother and his traveling cloak—two secret blessings, which, though many guessed at, nobody quite understood. Nor did they understand why he loved so the little upper room, except that it had been his mother's room, in the window of which, as people remembered now, she had used to sit for hours watching the Beautiful Mountains.

Out that window he used to fly—not very often. As he grew older, the labors of state prevented the frequent use of his traveling cloak; still he did use it sometimes. Only now it was less for his own pleasure and amusement than to see something or investigate something for the good of the country. But he prized his godmother's gift as dearly as ever. It was a comfort to him in all his vexations, an enhancement of all his joys. It made him almost forget his lameness—which was never cured.

However, the cruel things which had been once foreboded of him did not happen. His misfortune was not such a heavy one, after all. It proved to be of much less inconvenience, even to himself, than had been feared. A council of eminent surgeons and mechanicians invented for him a wonderful pair of crutches, with the help of which, though he never walked easily or gracefully, he did manage to walk so as to be quite independent. And such was the love his people bore him that they never heard the sound of his crutches on the marble palace floors without a leap of the heart, for they knew that good was coming to them whenever he approached.

Thus, though he never walked in processions, never reviewed his troops mounted on a magnificent charger, nor did any of the things which make a show monarch so much appreciated, he was able to perform all the duties and to enjoy a great many of the pleasures of his rank. When he held his levees, not standing, but seated on a throne ingeniously contrived to hide his infirmity, the people thronged to greet him. When he drove out through the city streets, shouts followed him wherever he went—

every countenance brightened as he passed, and his own, perhaps, was the brightest of all.

First, because, accepting his affliction as inevitable, he took it patiently; second, because, being a brave man, he bore it bravely, trying to forget himself, and live out of himself, and in and for other people. Therefore other people grew to love him so well that I think hundreds of his subjects might have been found who were almost ready to die for their poor lame king.

He never gave them a queen. When they implored him to choose one, he replied that his country was his bride, and he desired no other. But perhaps the real reason was that he shrank from any change; and that no wife in all the world would have been found so perfect, so lovable, so tender to him in all his weaknesses as his beautiful old godmother.

His twenty-four other godfathers and godmothers, or as many of them as were still alive, crowded round him as soon as he ascended the throne. He was very civil to them all, but adopted none of the names they had given him, keeping to the one by which he had been always known, though it had now almost lost its meaning; for King Dolor was one of the happiest and cheerfulest men alive.

He did a good many things, however, unlike most men and most kings, which a little astonished his subjects. First, he pardoned the condemned woman

who had been his nurse, and ordained that from
henceforth there should be no such thing as the punishment of death in Nomansland. All capital criminals were to be sent to perpetual imprisonment in

Hopeless Tower and the plain round about it, where they could do no harm to anybody, and might in time do a little good, as the woman had done.

Another surprise he shortly afterward gave the nation. He recalled his uncle's family, who had fled away in terror to another country, and restored them to all their honors. By and by he chose the eldest son of his eldest cousin (who had been dead a year), and had him educated in the royal palace, as the heir to the throne. This little prince was a quiet, unobtrusive boy, so that everybody wondered at the King's choosing him when there were so many more. But as he grew into a fine young fellow, good and brave, they agreed that the King had judged more wisely than they.

"Not a lame prince, either," his Majesty observed one day, watching him affectionately. For he was the best runner, the highest leaper, the keenest and most active sportsman in the country. "One cannot make one's self, but one can sometimes help a little in the making of somebody else. It is well."

This was said, not to any of his great lords and ladies, but to a good old woman—his first homely nurse—whom he had sought for far and wide, and at last had found in her cottage among the Beautiful Mountains. He sent for her to visit him once a year, and treated her with great honor until she died. He was equally kind, though somewhat less tender, to

his other nurse, who, after receiving her pardon, returned to her native town and grew into a great lady,
and I hope a good one. But as she was so grand a
personage now, any little faults she had did not
show.

Thus King Dolor's reign passed year after year,
long and prosperous. Whether he was happy—"as

happy as a king"—is a question no human being can
decide. But I think he was, because he had the power
of making everybody about him happy, and did it
too; also because he was his godmother's godson,
and could shut himself up with her whenever he
liked, in that quiet little room in view of the Beautiful Mountains, which nobody else ever saw or cared
to see. They were too far off, and the city lay so low.

But there they were, all the time. No change ever came to them; and I think, at any day throughout his long reign, the King would sooner have lost his crown than have lost sight of the Beautiful Mountains.

In course of time, when the little Prince his cousin was grown into a tall young man, capable of all the duties of a man, his Majesty did one of the most extraordinary acts ever known in a sovereign beloved by his people and prosperous in his reign. He announced that he wished to invest his heir with the royal purple—at any rate, for a time—while he himself went away on a distant journey, whither he had long desired to go.

Everybody marveled, but nobody opposed him. Who could oppose the good King, who was not a young king now? And besides, the nation had a great admiration for the young Regent—and possibly a lurking pleasure in change.

So there was a fixed day when all the people whom it would hold assembled in the great square of the capital, to see the young Prince installed solemnly in his new duties, and undertaking his new vows. He was a very fine young fellow; tall and straight as a poplar tree, with a frank, handsome face—a great deal handsomer than the King's, some people said, but others thought differently. However, as his Majesty sat on his throne, with his gray hair falling from

underneath his crown, and a few wrinkles showing
in spite of his smile, there was something about his
countenance which made his people, even while
they shouted, regard him with a tenderness mixed
with awe.

He lifted up his thin, slender hand, and there
came a silence over the vast crowd immediately.
Then he spoke, in his own accustomed way, using no
grand words, but saying what he had to say in the
simplest fashion, though with a clearness that struck
their ears like the first song of a bird in the dusk of
the morning.

The astonished people stood watching as the Prince floated away

"My people, I am tired; I want to rest. I have had a long reign, and done much work—at least, as much as I was able to do. Many might have done it better than I—but none with a better will. Now I leave it to others; I am tired, very tired. Let me go home."

There arose a murmur—of content or discontent none could well tell; then it died down again, and the assembly listened silently once more.

"I am not anxious about you, my people—my children," continued the King. "You are prosperous and at peace. I leave you in good hands. The Prince Regent will be a fitter king for you than I."

"No, no, no!" rose the universal shout—and those who had sometimes found fault with him shouted louder than anybody. But he seemed as if he heard them not.

"Yes, yes," said he, as soon as the tumult had a little subsided; and his voice sounded firm and clear. Some very old people, who boasted of having seen him as a child, declared that his face took a sudden change, and grew as young and sweet as that of the little Prince Dolor. "Yes, I must go. It is time for me to go. Remember me sometimes, my people, for I have loved you well. And I am going a long way, and I do not think I shall come back any more."

He drew a little bundle out of his breast pocket— a bundle that nobody had ever seen before. It was small and shabby-looking, and tied up with many knots, which untied themselves in an instant. With a joyful countenance, he muttered over it a few half-intelligible words. Then, so suddenly that even those nearest to his Majesty could not tell how it came about, the King was away—away—floating right up in the air—upon something, they knew not what, except that it appeared to be as safe and pleasant as the wings of a bird.

And after him sprang a bird—a dear little lark, rising from whence no one could say, since larks do not usually build their nests on the pavement of city squares. But there it was, a real lark, singing far over their heads, louder and clearer and more joyful as it vanished farther into the blue sky.

Shading their eyes, and straining their ears, the astonished people stood until the whole vision disappeared like a speck in the clouds—the rosy clouds that overhung the Beautiful Mountains.

King Dolor was never again beheld or heard of in his own country. But the good he had done there lasted for years and years. He was long missed and deeply mourned—at least, so far as anybody could mourn one who was gone on such a happy journey.

Whither he went, or who went with him, it is impossible to say. But I myself believe that his godmother took him on his traveling cloak to the Beautiful Mountains. What he did there, or where he is now, who can tell? I cannot. But one thing I am quite sure of, that, wherever he is, he is perfectly happy.

And so, when I think of him, am I.

THE
ADVENTURES
OF A
BROWNIE

ADVENTURE
THE FIRST

Brownie and the Cook

THERE WAS ONCE a little Brownie who lived—where do you think he lived?—in a coal cellar.

Now a coal cellar may seem a most curious place to choose to live in; but then a Brownie is a curious creature—a fairy, yet not one of that sort of fairies who fly about on gossamer wings, and dance in the moonlight, and so on. He never dances; and as to wings, what use would they be to him in a coal cellar? He is a sober, stay-at-home household elf—nothing much to look at, even if you did see him, which you are not likely to do. He is just a little old man, about a foot high, all dressed in brown, with a brown face and hands, and a brown peaked cap, exactly the color of a brown mouse. And like a mouse he hides in corners—especially kitchen corners, and comes out only after dark when nobody is about, and so sometimes people call him Mr. Nobody.

I said you were not likely to see him; I never did, certainly, and never knew anybody that did, but still, if you were to go into Devonshire, you would hear many funny stories about Brownies in general. So I may as well tell you the adventures of one particular Brownie, who belonged to a family there; which family he had followed from house to house, most faithfully, for years and years.

A good many people had heard him—or supposed they had—when there were extraordinary noises about the house; noises which must have come from a mouse or a rat—or a Brownie. But nobody had ever seen him, except the children, the three little boys and three little girls—who declared he often came to play with them when they were alone, and was the nicest companion in the world, though he was such an old man—hundreds of years old! He was full of fun and mischief, and up to all sorts of tricks; but he never did anybody any harm—unless they deserved it.

Brownie was supposed to live under one particular coal, in the darkest corner of the cellar, which was never allowed to be disturbed. Why he had chosen it nobody knew, and how he lived there nobody knew either; nor what he lived upon. Except that, ever since the family could remember, there had always been a bowl of milk put behind the coal-cellar door for the Brownie's supper. Perhaps he drank it —perhaps he didn't; anyhow, the bowl was always found empty next morning.

The old Cook, who had lived all her life in the family, had never once forgotten to give Brownie his supper. But at last she died, and a young Cook came in her stead, who was very apt to forget everything. She was also both careless and lazy, and disliked taking the trouble to put a bowl of milk in the same place every night for Mr. Nobody. "I don't believe in Brownies," she said; "I've never seen one, and seeing's believing." So she laughed at the other servants, who looked very grave and put the bowl of milk in its place as often as they could, without saying much about it.

But once, when Brownie woke up, at his usual hour for rising—ten o'clock at night—and looked round in search of his supper—which was in fact his breakfast—he found nothing there. At first he could not imagine such neglect, and went smelling and smelling about for his bowl of milk—it was not always placed in the same corner now—but in vain.

"This will never do," said he. And being extremely hungry, he began running about the coal cellar to see what he could find. His eyes were as useful in the dark as in the light—like a pussycat's; but there was nothing to be seen—not even a potato paring, or a dry crust, or a well-gnawed bone, such as Tiny the terrier sometimes brought into the coal cellar and left on the floor. Nothing, in short, but heaps of coals and coal dust; which even a Brownie cannot eat, you know.

"Can't stand this; quite impossible!" said the Brownie, tightening his belt to make his poor little inside feel less empty. He had been asleep so long—about a week, I believe, as was his habit when there was nothing to do—that he seemed ready to eat his own head, or his boots, or anything. "What's to be done? Since nobody brings my supper I must go and fetch it."

He spoke quickly, for he always thought quickly, and made up his mind in a minute. To be sure, it was a very little mind, like his little body; but he did the best he could with it, and was not a bad sort of old fellow after all. In the house he had never done any harm—and often some good, for he frightened away all the rats, mice, and black beetles. Not the crickets, however. He liked them, as the old Cook had done. She said they were such cheerful creatures, and always brought luck to the house. But the young Cook could not bear them, and used to pour boiling water down their holes, and set basins of beer with little wooden bridges up to the rim, that they might walk up, tumble in, and be drowned.

So there was not even a cricket singing in the silent house when Brownie put his head out of his coal-cellar door, which, to his surprise, he found open. Old Cook used to lock it every night; but the young Cook had left that key, and the kitchen and pantry keys too, all dangling in the lock, so that any thief might have got in, and wandered all over the house without being found out.

"Hurrah, here's luck!" cried Brownie, tossing his cap up in the air, and bounding right through the scullery into the kitchen. It was quite empty, but there was a good fire burning itself out, just for its own amusement, and the remains of a capital supper were spread on the table—enough for half a dozen people.

Would you like to know what there was? Devonshire cream, of course; and part of a large dish of junket, which is something like curds and whey. Lots of bread and butter and cheese, and half an apple pudding. Also a great jug of cider and another of milk, and several half-filled glasses, and no end of dirty plates, knives and forks. All were scattered about the table in the most untidy fashion, just as the servants had risen from their supper, without thinking to put anything away.

Brownie screwed up his little old face and turned

up his button of a nose, and gave a long whistle. You might not believe it, seeing he lived in a coal cellar, but really he liked tidiness, and always played his pranks upon disorderly or slovenly folk.

"Whew!" said he, "here's a chance! What a supper I'll get now!"

And he jumped onto a chair and thence to the table, but so quietly that the large black cat with four white paws (called Muff, because she was so

fat and soft and her fur so long), who sat dozing in front of the fire, just opened one eye and went to sleep again. She had tried to get her nose into the milk jug, but it was too small; and the junket dish was too deep for her to reach, except with one paw. She didn't care much for bread and cheese and apple pudding, and was very well fed besides. So after wandering round the table she had jumped down from it again, and settled herself to sleep on the hearth.

But Brownie had no notion of going to sleep. He wanted his supper, and oh! what a supper he did eat; first one thing and then another, and then trying everything all over again. And oh! what a lot he drank!—first milk and then cider, and then mixed the two together in a way that would have disagreed with anybody except a Brownie. As it was, he was obliged to slacken his belt several times, and at last took it off altogether. But he must have had a most extraordinary capacity for eating and drinking— since, after he had cleared off all the food, he was just as lively as ever, and begin jumping about on the table as if he had had no supper at all.

His jumping was a little unfortunate, for there happened to be a clean white tablecloth. As this was only Monday, it had had no time to get dirty— untidy as the Cook was. And you know Brownie lived in a coal cellar, and his feet were black with running about in coal dust. So wherever he trod he left the impression behind; until at last the whole tablecloth was covered with black marks.

Not that he minded this. In fact, he took great pains to make the cloth as dirty as possible; and then laughing loudly "Ho, ho, ho!" leaped onto the hearth, and began teasing the cat. He squeaked like a mouse, or chirped like a cricket, or buzzed like a fly; and altogether disturbed poor Pussy's mind so

much that she went and hid herself in the farthest corner, and left him the hearth all to himself, where he lay at ease till daybreak.

Then, hearing a slight noise overhead, which might be the servants getting up, he jumped onto the table again—gobbled up the few remaining crumbs for his breakfast, and scampered off to his coal cellar. Here he hid himself under his big coal, and fell asleep for the day.

Well, the Cook came downstairs rather earlier than usual, for she remembered she had to clear off the remains of supper. But lo and behold, there was nothing left to clear! Every bit of food was eaten up. The cheese looked as if a dozen mice had been nibbling at it, and nibbled it down to the very rind. The milk and cider were all gone—and mice don't care for milk and cider, you know. As for the apple pudding, it had vanished altogether; and the dish was licked as clean as if Boxer the yard dog had been at it, in his hungriest mood.

"And my white tablecloth—oh, my clean white tablecloth! What can have been done to it?" cried she in amazement. For little black footmarks were all over it, just the size of a baby's foot—only babies don't wear shoes with nails in them, and don't run about and climb on kitchen tables after all the family have gone to bed.

Cook was a little frightened; but her fright changed to anger when she saw the large black cat stretched comfortably on the hearth. Poor Muff had crept there for a little snooze after Brownie went away.

"You nasty cat! I see it all now. It's you that have eaten up all the supper; it's you that have been on my clean tablecloth with your dirty paws."

They were white paws, and as clean as possible; but Cook never thought of that, any more than she did of the fact that cats don't usually drink cider or eat apple pudding.

"I'll teach you to come stealing food in this way. Take that—and that—and that!"

Cook got hold of a broom and beat poor Pussy till the creature ran mewing away. She couldn't speak, you know—unfortunate cat! So she could not tell people that it was Brownie who had done it all.

Next night Cook thought she would make all safe and sure. So, instead of letting the cat sleep by the fire, she shut her up in the chilly coal cellar, locked the door, put the key in her pocket, and went off to bed; leaving the supper as before.

When Brownie woke up and looked out of his hole, there was as usual no supper for him, and the cellar door was shut. He peered about, to try and find some cranny under the door to creep through, but there was none. And he felt so hungry that he could almost have eaten the cat, who kept walking to and fro in a melancholy manner. Only she was alive, and he couldn't very well eat her alive. Besides he knew she was old, and had an idea she might be tough; so he merely said, politely, "How do you do, Mrs. Pussy?" to which she answered nothing—of course.

Something must be done, and luckily Brownies can do things which nobody else can do. So he thought he would change himself into a mouse, and gnaw a hole through the door. But then he suddenly remembered the cat, who, though he had decided not to eat her, might take this opportunity of eating him. So he thought it advisable to wait till she was fast asleep, which did not happen for a good while. At length, quite tired with walking about, Pussy turned round on her tail six times, curled down in a corner, and fell fast asleep.

Immediately Brownie changed himself into the smallest mouse possible. And, taking care not to make the least noise, he gnawed a hole in the door, and squeezed himself through—immediately turning into his proper shape again, for fear of accidents.

The kitchen fire was at its last glimmer; but there was a better supper than even last night, for the Cook had had friends with her, a brother and two cousins, and they had been exceedingly merry. The food they had left behind was enough for three Brownies, at least, but this one managed to eat it all up. Only once, in trying to cut a great slice of beef, he let the carving knife and fork fall with such a clatter that Tiny the terrier, who was tied up at the foot of the stairs, began to bark furiously. However, he brought her her puppy, which had been left in a basket in a corner of the kitchen, and so succeeded in quieting her.

After that he enjoyed himself amazingly, and made more marks than ever on the white tablecloth —for he began jumping about like a pea on a trencher, in order to make his particularly large supper agree with him.

Then, in the absence of the cat, he teased the puppy for an hour or two, till, hearing the clock strike five, he thought it as well to turn into a mouse again, and creep back cautiously into his cellar. He was only just in time, for Muff opened one eye and was just going to pounce upon him when he changed himself back into a Brownie. She was so startled that she bounded away, her tail growing into twice its natural size, and her eyes gleaming like round green globes. But Brownie only said, "Ha, ha, ho!" and walked deliberately into his hole.

When Cook came downstairs and saw that the same thing had happened again—that the supper was all eaten, and the tablecloth blacker than ever with the extraordinary footmarks, she was greatly puzzled. Who could have done it all? Not the cat, who came mewing out of the coal cellar the minute she unlocked the door. Possibly a rat—but then would a rat have come within reach of Tiny?

"It must have been Tiny herself, or her puppy," which just came rolling out of its basket over Cook's feet. "You little wretch! You and your mother are the greatest nuisance imaginable. I'll punish you!"

And quite forgetting that Tiny had been safely tied up all night, and that her poor little puppy was so fat and helpless it could scarcely stand on its legs —and so was unlikely to jump on chairs and tables, she gave them both such a thrashing that they ran howling together out 'he kitchen door, where the kind little kitchenmaid took them up in her arms.

"You ought to have beaten the Brownie, if you could catch him," said she indignantly. "He'll do it again and again, you'll see, for he can't bear an untidy kitchen. You'd better do as poor old Cook did, and clear the supper things away, and put the odds and ends safe in the larder. Also," she added mysteriously, "if I were you, I'd put a bowl of milk behind the coal-cellar door."

"Nonsense!" answered the young Cook, and flounced away. But afterwards she thought better of it, and did as she was advised, grumbling all the time, but doing it.

Next morning, the milk was gone! Perhaps Brownie had drunk it up, anyhow nobody could say that he hadn't. As for the supper, Cook having safely laid it on the shelves of the larder, nobody touched it. And the tablecloth, which was wrapped up tidily and put in the dresser drawer, came out as clean as ever, with not a single black footmark upon it. No mischief being done, the cat and the dog both escaped beating, and Brownie played no more tricks with anybody—till the next time.

ADVENTURE
THE SECOND

Brownie and the Cherry Tree

THE "NEXT TIME" was quick in coming, which was not wonderful, considering there was a Brownie in the house. Otherwise the house was like most other houses, and the family like most other families. The children also: they were sometimes good, sometimes naughty, like other children. But on the whole they deserved to have the pleasure of a Brownie to play with them, as they declared he did—many and many a time.

A favorite play place was the orchard, where grew the biggest cherry tree you ever saw. They called it their "castle," because it rose up ten feet from the ground in one thick stem, and then branched out into a circle of boughs, with a flat place in the middle, where two or three children could sit at a time. There they often did sit, turn by turn, or one at a time—sometimes with a book, reading. And the biggest boy made a sort of rope ladder by which they could climb up and down—which they did all winter, and enjoyed their "castle" very much.

But one day in spring they found their ladder cut away! The Gardener had done it, saying it injured the tree, which was just coming into blossom. Now this Gardener was a rather gruff man, with a growling voice. He did not mean to be unkind, but he disliked children. He said they bothered him. But when they complained to their mother about the ladder, she agreed with Gardener that the tree must not be injured, as it bore the biggest cherries in all the neighborhood—so big that the old saying of "taking two bites at a cherry" came really true.

"Wait till the cherries are ripe," said she. And so the little people waited, and watched it through its leafing and blossoming—such sheets of blossom, white as snow!—till the fruit began to show, and grew large and red on every bough.

At last one morning the mother said, "Children, would you like to help gather the cherries today?"

"Hurrah!" they cried, "and not a day too soon; for we saw a flock of starlings in the next field—and if we don't clear the tree they will."

"Very well; clear it then. Only mind and fill my basket quite full for preserving. What is left over you may eat if you like."

"Thank you, thank you," and the children were eager to be off, but the mother stopped them till she could get the Gardener and his ladder.

"For it is he who must climb the tree, not you. And you must do exactly as he tells you; for he will stay with you all the time and see that you don't come to any harm."

This was no slight cloud on the children's happiness, and they begged hard to go alone.

"Please might we? We will be so good!"

The mother shook her head. All the goodness in the world would not help them if they tumbled off the tree or ate themselves sick with cherries.

"You would not be safe, and I would be too unhappy."

To make mother "unhappy" was the worst rebuke possible to these children; so they choked down their disappointment, and followed the Gardener as he walked on ahead, carrying his ladder on his shoulder. He looked very cross, and as if he did not like the children's company at all.

They were pretty good on the whole, though they chattered a good deal. But the Gardener said not a word to them all the way to the orchard. When they reached it he just told them to "keep out of his way and not worrit him," which they politely promised, saying among themselves that they should not enjoy their cherry gathering at all. But children who make the best of things, and try to be as good as they can, sometimes have fun unawares.

When the Gardener was steadying his ladder against the trunk of the cherry tree, there was suddenly heard the barking of a dog, and a very fierce dog, too. First it seemed close beside them, then in the flower garden, then in the fowl yard.

Gardener dropped the ladder out of his hands. "It's that Boxer! He has got loose again! He will be running after my chickens, and dragging his broken chain all over my borders. And he is so fierce, and so delighted to get free. He'll bite anybody who ties him up, except me."

"Hadn't you better go and look after him?"

Gardener thought it was the eldest boy who spoke, and turned round angrily; but the little fellow had never opened his lips.

Now there was heard a still louder bark, and from a quite different part of the garden.

"There he is—I'm sure of it! Jumping over my bedding-out plants, and breaking my cucumber frames. Abominable beast!—just let me catch him!"

Off Gardener darted in a violent passion, throwing the ladder down upon the grass, and forgetting all about the cherries and the children.

The instant he was gone, a shrill laugh, loud and merry, was heard close by, and a little brown old man's face peeped from behind the cherry tree.

"How d'ye do?—Boxer was me. Didn't I bark well? Now I've come to play with you."

The children clapped their hands. For they knew they were going to have some fun if Brownie was there—he was the best little playfellow in the world. And then they had him all to themselves. Nobody ever saw him except the children.

"Come on!" cried he, in his shrill voice, half like an old man's, half like a baby's. "Who'll begin to gather the cherries?"

They all looked blank, for the tree was so high to where the branches began, and besides, their mother had said they were not to climb. And the ladder lay flat upon the grass—far too heavy for little hands to move.

"What! you big boys don't expect a poor little fellow like me to lift the ladder all by myself? Try! I'll help you."

Whether he helped or not, no sooner had they taken hold of the ladder than it rose up, almost of its own accord, and fixed itself quite safely against the tree.

"But we must not climb; mother told us not to," said the boys ruefully. "Mother said we were to stand at the bottom and pick up the cherries."

"Very well. Obey your mother. I'll just run up the tree myself."

Before the words were out of his mouth Brownie had darted up the ladder like a monkey, and disappeared among the fruit-laden branches.

The children looked dismayed for a minute, till they saw a merry brown face peeping out from the green leaves at the very top of the tree.

"Biggest fruit always grows highest," cried the Brownie. "Stand in a row, all you children. Little boys, hold out your caps. Little girls, make a bag of your pinafores. Open your mouths and shut your eyes, and see what the Queen will send you."

They laughed and did as they were told; whereupon they were drowned in a shower of cherries—cherries falling like hailstones, hitting them on their heads, their cheeks, their noses—filling their caps and pinafores, and then rolling and tumbling onto the grass, till it was strewn thick as leaves in autumn with the rosy fruit.

What a glorious scramble they had!—these three little boys and three little girls. How they laughed and jumped and knocked heads together in picking up the cherries—yet never quarreled, for there were such heaps it would have been ridiculous to squabble over them. And besides, whenever they began to quarrel, Brownie always ran away. Now he was the merriest of the lot. He ran up and down the tree like a cat, helped to pick up the cherries, and was first rate at filling the large market basket.

"We were to eat as many as we liked, only we must first fill the basket," conscientiously said the eldest girl; upon which they all set to at once, and filled it to the brim.

"Now we'll have a dinner party," cried the Brownie. He squatted down like a Turk, crossing his queer little legs, and sticking his elbows upon his knees, in a way that nobody but a Brownie could manage. "Sit in a ring! Sit in a ring! And we'll see who can eat fastest."

The children obeyed. How many cherries they devoured, and how fast they did it, passes my capacity for telling. I only hope they were not ill next day —and that all the cherry stones they swallowed by mistake did not disagree with them. But perhaps nothing does disagree with one when one dines with a Brownie.

They ate so much, laughing in equal proportion, that they had quite forgotten the Gardener—when all of a sudden they heard him clicking angrily the orchard gate, and talking to himself as he walked through.

"That nasty dog! It wasn't Boxer after all! A nice joke! To find him quietly asleep in his kennel—after having hunted him, as I thought, from one end of the garden to the other! Now for the cherries and the

children—Bless us, where are the children? And the
cherries! Why, the tree is as bare as a blackthorn in
February! The starlings have been at it, after all. Oh,
dear! Oh, dear!"

"Oh, dear! Oh, dear!" echoed a voice from behind
the tree, followed by shouts of mocking laughter.
Not from the children—they sat as demure as possible, all in a ring, with their hands before them, and
in the center the huge basket of cherries, piled as full
as it could possibly hold. But the Brownie had disappeared.

"You naughty brats, I'll have you punished!" cried
the Gardener, furious at the laughter, for he never
laughed himself. But as there was nothing wrong—
the cherries being gathered, a very large crop, and
the ladder found safe in its place—it was difficult to
say what had been the harm done and who had done
it.

So he went growling back to the house, carrying
the cherries to the mistress, who coaxed him into
good temper again, as she sometimes did; bidding
also the children to behave well to him, since he was
an old man, and not really bad—only cross. As for
the little folks, she had not the slightest intention of
punishing them; and as for Brownie, it was impossible to catch him. So nobody was punished at all.

ADVENTURE
THE THIRD

Brownie in the Farmyard

THE FARMYARD WAS a place where Brownie did not often go, for he preferred being warm and snug in the house. But when he felt himself ill-used, he would wander anywhere, in order to play tricks upon those who he thought had done him harm. For being only a Brownie, and not a man, he did not understand that the best way to revenge yourself upon your enemies is either to let them alone or to pay them back good for evil; which disappoints them so much and makes them so exceedingly ashamed of themselves.

One day Brownie overheard the Gardener advising the Cook to put into his bowl at night sour milk instead of sweet.

"He'd never find out the difference, no more than the pigs do. Indeed it's my belief that a pig, or dog, or something, empties the bowl, and not a Brownie at all. It's just clean waste—that's what I say."

"Then you'd better hold your tongue, and mind your own business," returned the Cook, who had a sharp temper and would not stand being meddled with. She began to abuse the Gardener soundly. But his wife, who was standing by, took his part, as she always did when any third party scolded him. So they squabbled together, till Brownie, hiding under his coal, put his little hands over his little ears.

"Dear me, what a noise these mortals do make when they quarrel! They quite deafen me. I must teach them better manners."

But when the Cook slammed the door, and left Gardener and his wife alone, they two began to dispute between themselves.

"You make such a fuss over your nasty pigs, and get all the scraps for them," said the wife. "It's of much more importance that I should have everything Cook can spare for my chickens. Never were there such fine chickens as my last brood!"

"I thought they were ducklings."

"How you catch me up, you rude old man! They are ducklings, and beauties too—even though they

have never seen water. Where's the pond you promised to make for me, I wonder?"

"Rubbish, woman! If my cows do without a pond,
your ducklings may. And why will you be so silly as
to rear ducklings at all? Fine fat chickens are a deal
better. You'll find out your mistake someday!"

"And so will you when that old Alderney runs
dry. You'll wish you had taken my advice and fat-
tened and sold her."

"Alderney cows don't sell for fattening. Women's
advice is never worth twopence. Yours isn't worth
even a halfpenny. What are you laughing at?"

"I wasn't laughing," said the wife angrily. And in
truth it was not she, but little Brownie, who ran under the barrow which the Gardener was wheeling
along, very much amused that human beings should
be so silly as to squabble about nothing.

It was still early morning; for whatever this old
couple's faults might be, laziness was not one of
them. The wife rose with the dawn to feed her poul-
try and collect her eggs. The husband also got
through as much work by breakfast time as many an
idle man does by noon. But Brownie had been be-
forehand with them this day.

When all the fowls came running to be fed, the
big Brahma hen who had hatched the ducklings was
seen wandering forlornly about, and clucking
mournfully for her young brood—she could not find

them anywhere. Had she been able to speak, she might have told how a large white Aylesbury duck had waddled into the farmyard, and waddled out again, coaxing them after her, no doubt in search of a pond. But missing they were, most certainly.

"Cluck, cluck, cluck!" mourned the miserable hen-mother—and "Oh, my ducklings, my ducklings!"

cried the Gardener's wife—"Who can have carried off my beautiful ducklings?"

"Rats, maybe," said the Gardener cruelly, as he walked away. And as he went he heard the squeak of a rat below his wheelbarrow. But he could not catch it, any more than his wife could catch the Aylesbury duck. Of course not. Both were—the Brownie!

Just at this moment the six little people came run-

They were drowned in a shower of cherries

ning into the farmyard. When they had been particularly good, they were sometimes allowed to go
with Gardener a-milking, each carrying his or her
own mug for a drink of milk, warm from the cow.
They scampered after him—a noisy tribe, begging to
be taken down to the field, and holding out their
six mugs entreatingly.

"What, six cupfuls of milk, when I haven't a drop
to spare, and Cook is always wanting more? Ridiculous nonsense! Get along with you. You may come
to the field—I can't hinder that—but you'll get no
milk this day. Take your mugs back again to the
kitchen."

The poor little folks made the best of a bad business, and obeyed; then followed Gardener down to
the field rather dolefully. But it was such a beautiful
morning that they soon recovered their spirits. The
grass shone with dew, like a sheet of diamonds, the
clover smelt so sweet, and two skylarks were singing at each other high up in the sky. Several rabbits darted past, to their great amusement, especially one very large rabbit, brown, not gray, which
dodged in and out among them, and once nearly
threw Gardener down, pail and all, by running
across his feet—which set them all laughing till they
came where Dolly the cow lay chewing her cud under a large oak tree.

It was great fun to stir her up—as usual—and lie down, one after the other, in the place where she had lain all night long, making the grass flat, and warm and perfumy with her sweet breath. She let them do it, and then stood meekly by; for Dolly was the gentlest cow in the world.

But this morning something strange seemed to possess her. She altogether refused to be milked— kicked, plunged, tossed over the pail, which was luckily empty.

"Bless the cow! what's wrong with her? It's surely you children's fault. Stand off, the whole lot of you. Soh, Dolly! good Dolly!"

But Dolly was anything but good. She stood, switching her tail and looking as savage as so mild an animal possibly could look.

"It's all your doing, you naughty children! You've been playing her some trick, I know," cried the Gardener in great wrath.

They assured him they had done nothing, and indeed they looked as quiet as mice and as innocent as lambs. At length the biggest boy pointed out a large wasp which had settled in Dolly's ear.

"That accounts for everything," said the Gardener.

But it did not mend everything. For when he tried to drive it away it kept coming back and back again, and buzzing round his own head, and the cow's, with a voice that the children thought was less like the buzz of a wasp than the sound of a person laughing. At length it frightened Dolly to such an extent that with one wild bound she darted right away, and galloped off to the farther end of the field.

"I'll get a rope and tie her legs together," cried the Gardener fiercely. "She shall repent giving me all this trouble—that she shall!"

"Ha, ha, ha!" laughed somebody. The Gardener thought it was the children, and gave one of them an angry cuff as he walked away. But they knew it was somebody else, and were not at all surprised when, the minute his back was turned, Dolly came walking quietly back, led by a little wee brown man who scarcely reached up to her knees. Yet she let him guide her, which he did as gently as possible, though the string he held her by was no thicker than a spider-web, floating from one of her horns.

"Soh, Dolly! good Dolly!" cried Brownie, mimicking the Gardener's voice. "Now we'll see what we can do. I want my breakfast badly—don't you, little folks?"

Of course they did, for the morning air made them very hungry.

"Very well—wait a bit, though. Old people should be served first, you know. Besides, I want to go to bed."

Go to bed in the daylight! The children all laughed, and then looked quite shy and sorry, lest they might have seemed rude to the Brownie. But he—he liked fun; and never took offense when none was meant.

He placed himself on the milking stool, which was so high that his little legs were dangling half-way down, and milked and milked—Dolly standing as still as possible—till he had filled the whole pail. Most astonishing cow! she gave as much as two cows—and such delicious milk as it was—all frothing and yellow—richer than even Dolly's milk had ever been before. The children's mouths watered for it, but not a word said they—even when, instead of giving it to them, Brownie put his own mouth to the pail, and drank and drank, till it seemed as if he were never going to stop. But it was decidedly a relief to them when he popped his head up again, and lo! the pail was as full as ever!

"Now, little ones, now's your turn. Where are your mugs?"

All answered mournfully, "We've got none. Gardener made us take them back again."

"Never mind—all right. Gather me half a dozen of the biggest buttercups you can find."

"What nonsense!" thought the children; but they did it. Brownie laid the flowers in a row upon the eldest girl's lap—blew upon them one by one, and each turned into the most beautiful golden cup that ever was seen!

"Now, then, everyone take his own mug, and I'll fill it."

He milked away—each child got a drink, and then the cups were filled again. And all the while Dolly stood as quiet as possible—looking benignly round, as if she would be happy to supply milk to the whole parish, if the Brownie desired it.

"Soh, Dolly! Thank you, Dolly!" said he again, mimicking the Gardener's voice, half growling, half coaxing. And while he spoke, the real voice was heard behind the hedge. There was a sound as of a great wasp flying away, which made Dolly prick up her ears, and look as if the old savageness was coming back upon her. The children snatched up their mugs, but there was no need, they had all turned into buttercups again.

Gardener jumped over the stile, as cross as two sticks, with an old rope in his hand.

"Oh, what a bother I've had! Breakfast ready, and no milk yet—and such a row as they are making over

those lost ducklings. Stand back, you children, and don't hinder me a minute. No use begging—not a drop of milk shall you get. Hillo, Dolly! Quiet, old girl!"

Quiet enough she was this time—but you might as well have milked a plaster cow in a London milkshop. Not one ringing drop resounded against the empty pail; for, when they peeped in, the children saw to their amazement that it was empty.

"The creature's bewitched!" cried the Gardener in a great fury. "Or else somebody has milked her dry already. Have you done it? Or you?" he asked each of the children.

They might have said No—which was the literal truth—but then it would not have been the whole truth, for they knew quite well that Dolly had been milked, and also who had done it. And their mother had always taught them that to make a person believe a lie is nearly as bad as telling him one. Yet they did not like to betray the kind little Brownie. Greatly puzzled, they hung their heads and said nothing.

"Look in your pail again," cried a voice from the other side of Dolly. And there at the bottom was just the usual quantity of milk—no more and no less.

The Gardener was very much astonished. "It must be the Brownie!" muttered he in a frightened tone. And, taking off his hat, "Thank you, sir," said he to Mr. Nobody—at which the children all burst out laughing. But they kept their own counsel, and he was afraid to ask them any more questions.

By-and-by his fright wore off a little. "I only hope the milk is good, and will poison nobody," said he sulkily. "However, that's not my affair. You children had better tell your mother all about it. I left her in the farmyard in a pretty state of mind about her ducklings."

Perhaps Brownie heard this, and was sorry, for he

liked the children's mother, who had always been kind to him. Besides, he never did anybody harm who did not deserve it. And though, being a Brownie, he could hardly be said to have a conscience; he had something which stood in the place of one, a liking to see people happy rather than miserable.

So, instead of going to bed under his big coal for the day, when, after breakfast, the children and their mother came out to look at a new brood of chickens, he crept after them, and hid behind the hencoop where the old mother hen had been put with her young ones round her.

There had been great difficulty in getting her in there, for she was a hen who hatched her brood on independent principles. Instead of sitting upon the nice nest that the Gardener had made for her, she had twice gone into a little wood close by and made a nest for herself, which nobody could ever find. Here she hatched in secret, coming home every second day to be fed; and then vanishing again, till at last she reappeared in triumph, with her chickens running after her. The first brood there had been twelve, but this time there were fourteen—all from her own eggs, of course, and she was uncommonly proud of them. So was the Gardener, so was the mistress—who liked all young creatures. Such a

picture these were! Fourteen soft, yellow, fluffy
things—running about after their mother. It had
been a most troublesome business to catch—first her,
and then them, to put all under the coop. The old
hen resisted, and pecked furiously at Gardener's
legs, and the chickens ran about in frantic terror,
chirping wildly in answer to her clucking.

At last, however, the little family was safe in
shelter, and the chickens were counted again to see
that none had been lost in the scuffle. How funny
they were! Looking so innocent and yet so wise, as
chickens do—peering out at the world from under
their mother's wing, or hopping over her back, or
snuggled all together under her breast, so that noth-

ing could be seen of them but a mass of yellow legs, like a great centipede.

"How happy the old hen is," said the children's mother, looking on, and then looking compassionately at that other forlorn old hen, who had hatched the ducklings, and kept wandering about the farmyard, clucking miserably. "Those poor ducklings, what can have become of them? If rats had killed them we should have found feathers or something. And weasels would have sucked their brains and left them. They must have been stolen, or wandered away, and died of cold and hunger—my poor ducklings!"

The mistress sighed, for she could not bear any living thing to suffer. And the children nearly cried at the thought of what might be happening to their pretty ducklings. That very minute a little wee brown face was peering through a hole in the hencoop, making the old mother hen fly furiously at it —as she did at the slightest shadow of an enemy to her little ones.

However, no harm happened—only a guinea fowl suddenly ran across the farmyard, screaming in its usual harsh voice. But it was not the usual sort of guinea fowl, being larger and handsomer than any of theirs.

"Oh, what a beauty of a creature! How did it ever

come into our farmyard?" cried the delighted children; and started off after it, to catch it if possible.

But they ran and they ran—through the gate and out into the lane; and the guinea fowl still ran on before them, until turning round a corner they lost sight of it, and immediately saw something else, equally curious.

Sitting on the top of a big thistle—so big that he must have had to climb it just like a tree—was the Brownie. His legs were crossed, and his arms too; his little brown cap was stuck knowingly on one side, and he was laughing heartily.

"How do you do? Here I am again. I thought I wouldn't go to bed after all. Shall I help you to find the ducklings? Very well! come along."

They crossed the field, Brownie running beside them and as fast as he could, though he looked such an old man; and sometimes turning over on legs and arms like a Catherine wheel—which they tried to imitate, but generally failed, and only bruised their fingers and noses.

He lured them on and on till they came to the wood, and to a green path in it, which, well as they knew the neighborhood, none of the children had ever seen before. It led to a most beautiful pond, as clear as crystal and as blue as the sky. Large trees grew round it, dipping their branches in the water, as if they were looking at themselves in a glass. And all about their roots were quantities of primroses—the biggest primroses the children had ever seen.

Down they dropped on their fat knees, squashing down more primroses than they gathered, though they tried to gather them all. And the smallest child even began to cry because her hands were so full that the flowers dropped through her fingers.

But the boys, older and more practical, rather despised primroses.

"I thought we had come to look for ducklings," said the eldest. "Mother is fretting dreadfully about her ducklings. Where can they be?"

"Shut your eyes and you'll see," said the Brownie, at which they all laughed, but did as he had ordered. And when they opened their eyes again, what should they behold but a whole fleet of ducklings, sailing out from the roots of an old willow tree, one after the other, looking as fat and content as possible, and swimming as naturally as if they had lived on a pond, and this particular pond, all their days.

"Count them," said the Brownie, "the whole eight —quite correct. And then try and catch them—if you can."

Easier said than done. The boys set to work with great satisfaction—boys do so enjoy hunting some-

thing. They coaxed them—they shouted at them—
they threw little sticks at them. But as soon as they
wanted them to go one way the fleet of ducklings
immediately turned round and sailed another way,
doing it so deliberately and majestically that the
children could not help laughing. As for little
Brownie, he sat on a branch of the willow tree, with
his legs dangling down to the surface of the pond,
kicking at the water spiders and grinning with all
his might.

At length, quite tired out, in spite of their fun, the
children begged for his help, and he took compassion on them.

"Turn round three times and see what you can
find," shouted he.

Immediately each little boy found in his arms, and
each little girl in her pinafore, a fine fat duckling.
And there being eight of them, the two elder children had each a couple. They were rather cold and
damp, and slightly uncomfortable to cuddle, ducks
not being used to cuddling. Poor things! they strug-
gled hard to get away. But the children hugged them
tight, and ran as fast as their legs could carry them
through the wood, forgetting in their joy even to say
"Thank you" to the little Brownie.

When they reached their mother she was as glad
as they, for she had never thought to see her duck-

lings again. And to have them back all alive and un-injured, and watch them running to the old hen, who received them with an ecstasy of delight, was so exciting that nobody thought of asking a single question as to where they had been found.

When the mother did ask, the children told her all about Brownie's taking them to the beautiful pond—and what a wonderful pond it was: how green the trees were round it; and how large the primroses grew. They never tired of talking about it, and seeking for it. But the odd thing was that, seek as they might, they never could find it again. Many a day did the little people roam about, one by one or all together, round the wood, and across the wood, and up and down the wood, often getting themselves sadly draggled with mud, and torn with brambles; but the beautiful pond they never found again.

Nor did the ducklings, I suppose. For they wandered no more from the farmyard, to the old mother hen's great content. They grew up into fat and respectable ducks—five white ones and three gray ones —waddling about, very content, though they never saw water, except the tank which was placed for them to paddle in. They lived a lazy, peaceful, pleasant life for a long time, and were at last killed and eaten with green peas, one after the other, to the family's great satisfaction if not to their own.

ADVENTURE THE FOURTH

Brownie's Ride

THE LITTLE BROWNIE, though not given to horsemanship, did once take a ride, and a very remarkable one it was. Shall I tell you all about it?

The six little children got a present of something they had longed for all their lives—a pony. Not a rocking horse, but a real live pony—a Shetland pony, too, which had traveled all the way from the Shetland Isles to Devonshire—where everybody wondered at it, for such a creature had not been seen in the neighborhood for years and years. She was no bigger than a donkey, and her coat, instead of being smooth like a horse's, was shaggy, like a young bear's.

She had a long tail, which had never been cut, and such a deal of hair in her mane and over her eyes that it gave her quite a fierce countenance. In fact, among the mild and tame Devonshire beasts, the little Shetland pony looked almost like a wild animal.

But in reality she was the gentlest creature in the world. Before she had been many days with them, she began to know the children quite well. She followed them about, ate corn out of the bowl they held out to her; nay, one day when the eldest little girl offered her bread and butter, she stooped her head and took it from the child's hand, just like a young lady. Indeed, Jess—that was her name—was altogether so ladylike in her behavior that more than once Cook allowed her to walk in at the back door, where she stood politely warming her nose at the kitchen fire for a minute or two, then turned round and as politely walked out again. But she never did any mischief; and was so quiet and gentle a creature that she bade fair soon to become as great a pet in the household as the dog, the cat, the kittens, the puppies, the fowls, the ducks, the cow, the pig, and all the other members of the family.

The only one who disliked her, and grumbled at her, was the Gardener. This was odd; because, though cross to children, the old man was kind to dumb beasts. Even his pig knew his voice and grunted, and held out his nose to be scratched, and he always gave each successive pig a name, Jack or Dick, and called them by it, and was quite affectionate to them, one after the other, until the very day that they were killed. But they were English

pigs—and the pony was Scotch, and the Devonshire Gardener hated everything Scotch, he said. Besides, he was not used to groom's work, and the pony required such a deal of grooming on account of her long hair. More than once Gardener threatened to clip it short, and turn her into a regular English pony; but the children were in such distress at this that the mistress and mother forbade any such spoiling of Jess's personal appearance.

At length, to keep things smooth, and to avoid the rough words and even blows which poor Jess sometimes got, they sought in the village for a boy to look after her, and found a great rough shockheaded lad named Bill, who for a few shillings a week consented to come up every morning and learn the beginning of a groom's business. It was his hope to end, as his mother said he should, in sitting, like the squire's fat coachman, as broad as he was long, on the top of the hammercloth of a grand carriage, and do nothing all day but drive a pair of horses as stout as himself a few miles along the road and back again.

Bill would have liked this very much, he thought, if he could have been a coachman all at once, for if there was one thing he disliked it was work. He much preferred to lie in the sun all day and do nothing. He only agreed to come and take care of Jess because she was such a very little pony that looking after her seemed next door to doing nothing. But when he tried it he found his mistake. True, Jess was a very gentle beast; so quiet that the old mother hen with fourteen chicks used, instead of roosting with the rest of the fowls, to come regularly into the portion of the cowshed which was partitioned off for a stable, and settle under a corner of Jess's manger for the night; and in the morning the chicks would be seen running about fearlessly among her feet and under her very nose.

But for all that she required a little management, for she did not like her long hair to be roughly handled. It took a long time to clean her, and though she did not scream out like some silly little children when her hair was combed, I am afraid she sometimes kicked and bounced about, giving Bill a deal of trouble—all the more trouble, the more impatient Bill was.

And then he had to keep within call, for the children wanted their pony at all hours. She was their own especial property, and they insisted upon learning to ride—even before they got a saddle. Hard work it was to stick on Jess's bare back, but by degrees the boys did it, turn and turn about, and even gave their sisters a turn, too—a very little one—just once around the field and back again, which was quite enough, they considered, for girls. But they were very kind to their little sisters, held them on so that they could not fall, and led Jess carefully and quietly; and altogether behaved as elder brothers should.

Nor did they squabble very much among themselves, though sometimes it was rather difficult to keep their turns all fair, and remember accurately which was which. But they did their best, being on the whole extremely good children. And they were so happy to have their pony that they would have been ashamed to quarrel over her.

Also, one very curious thing kept them on their good behavior. Whenever they did begin to misconduct themselves, to want to ride out of their turns, or to domineer over one another, or the boys, joining together, tried to domineer over the girls, as I grieve to say boys not seldom do, they used to hear in the air, right over their heads, the crack of an unseen whip. It was not theirs, for none of them had got a whip. That was a felicity which their father had promised when they could all ride like young gentlemen and ladies. But there was no mistaking the sound—indeed, it always startled Jess so much that she set off galloping, and could not be caught again for many minutes.

This happened several times, until one of them said, "Perhaps it's the Brownie." Whether it was or not, it made them behave better for a good while: till one unfortunate day the two eldest began contending which should ride foremost and which hindmost on Jess's back, when "Crick—crack!" went the whip in the air, frightening the pony so much that she kicked up her heels, tossed both the boys over her head, and scampered off, followed by a loud "Ha, ha, ha!"

—Which certainly did not come from the two boys. They had fallen—quite safely, but rather unpleasantly—into a large nettle bed; whence they crawled out, rubbing their arms and legs, and looking too much ashamed to complain. But they were rather frightened and a little cross, for Jess took a skittish fit, and refused to be caught or mounted again, till the bell rang for school—when she grew as meek as possible. Too late—for the children were obliged to run indoors, and got no more rides for the whole day.

Jess was from this incident supposed to be on the same friendly terms with Brownie as were the rest of the household. Indeed, when she came, the children had taken care to lead her up to his coal-cellar door and introduce her to him properly—for Brownie was very jealous of strangers and often played them

tricks. But after that piece of civility he would be sure, they thought, to take her under his protection. And sometimes, when the little Shetlander was restless and pricked up her ears, looking preternaturally wise under those shaggy brows of hers, the children used to say to one another, "Perhaps she sees the Brownie."

Whether she did or not, Jess sometimes seemed to see a good deal that others did not see, and was apparently a favorite with the Brownie, for she grew and thrived so much that she soon became the pride and delight of the children and of the whole family. You would hardly have known her for the rough, shaggy, half-starved little beast that had arrived a few weeks before. Her coat was so silky, her limbs so graceful, and her head so full of intelligence that everybody admired her. Then, even Gardener began to admire her too.

"I think I'll get upon her back; it will save me walking down to the village," said he one day. And she actually carried him—though, as his feet nearly touched the ground, it looked as if the man were carrying the pony and not the pony the man. And the children laughed so immoderately that he never tried it afterwards.

Nor Bill neither, though he had once thought he should like a ride, and got astride on Jess—but she quickly ducked her head down, and he tumbled over it. Evidently she had her own tastes as to her riders, and much preferred little people to big ones.

Pretty Jess! When cantering round the paddock with the young folk, she really was quite a picture. And when at last she got a saddle—a new, beautiful saddle, with a pommel to take off and on, so as to suit both boys and girls—how proud they all were,

Jess included! That day they were allowed to take her into the market town—Gardener leading her, as Bill could not be trusted—and everybody, even the blacksmith, who hoped by-and-by to have the pleasure of shoeing her, said what a beautiful pony she was!

After this, Gardener treated Jess a great deal better, and showed Bill how to groom her, and kept him close at it too, which Bill did not like at all. He was a very lazy lad, and whenever he could shirk work he did it. Many a time when the children wanted Jess, either there was nobody to saddle her, or she had not been properly groomed, or Bill was away at his dinner, and they had to wait till he came back and could put her in order to be taken out for a ride like a genteel animal—which I am afraid neither pony nor children enjoyed half so much as the old ways before Bill came.

Still they were gradually becoming excellent little horsemen and horsewomen, even the youngest, only four years old, whom all the rest were very tender over, and who was often held on Jess's back and given a ride out of her turn because she was a good little girl and never cried for it. And seldomer and seldomer was heard the mysterious sound of the whip in the air, which warned them against quarreling—Brownie hated quarreling.

In fact, their only trouble was Bill, who never

came to his work on time, and never did things when wanted, and was ill-natured, lazy, and cross to the children, so that they disliked him very much.

"I wish the Brownie would punish you," said one of the boys; "you'd behave better then."

"The Brownie!" cried Bill contemptuously, "if I caught him I'd kick him up in the air, like this!"

And he kicked up his cap—his only cap, it was— which, strange to relate, flew right up, ever so high, and lodged at the very top of a tree which overhung the stable, where it dangled for weeks and weeks, during which time poor Bill had to go bareheaded.

He was very much vexed, and revenged himself by vexing the children in all sorts of ways. They would have told their mother, and asked her to send Bill away, only she had a great many anxieties just then, for their dear old grandmother was very ill, and they did not like to make a fuss about anything that would trouble her.

So Bill stayed on, and nobody found out what a bad, ill-natured, lazy boy he was.

But one day the mother was sent for suddenly by her mother. She did not know when she should be able to come home again. She was very sad, and so were the children, for they loved their grandmother —and as the carriage drove off they all stood crying round the front door for ever so long.

The servants even cried too—all but Bill.

"It's an ill wind that blows nobody good," said he. "What a jolly time I shall have! I'll do nothing all day

long. Those troublesome children shan't have Jess to ride. I'll keep her in the stable and then she won't get dirty, and I shall have no trouble in cleaning her. Hurrah! what fun!"

He put his hands in his pockets, and sat whistling the best part of the afternoon.

The children had been so unhappy that for that day they quite forgot Jess; but next morning after lessons were over, they came begging for a ride.

"You can't get one. The stable door's locked, and I've lost the key." (He had it in his pocket all the time.)

"How is poor Jess to get her dinner?" cried a thoughtful little girl. "Oh, how hungry she will be!"

And the child was quite in distress, as were the two other girls. But the boys were more angry than sorry.

"It was very stupid of you, Bill, to lose the key. Look about and find it, or else break open the door."

"I won't," said Bill. "I dare say the key will turn up before night, and if it doesn't—who cares? You get riding enough and too much. I'll not bother myself about it, or Jess either."

And Bill sauntered away. He was a big fellow, and the little lads were rather afraid of him. But as he walked, he could not keep his hand out of his trousers pocket, where the key felt as though it were growing heavier and heavier, till he expected it every minute to tumble through, and come out at his boots—convicting him before all the children of having told a lie.

Nobody was in the habit of telling lies to them,

so they never suspected him, but went innocently searching about for the key—Bill all the while clutching it fast. But every time he touched it, he felt his fingers pinched, as if there was a cockroach in his pocket—or a little lobster—or something, anyhow, that had claws. At last, fairly frightened, he made an excuse to go into the cowshed, took the key out of his pocket and looked at it, and finally hid it in a corner of the manger, amidst the hay.

As he did so, he heard a most extraordinary laugh, which was certainly not from Dolly the cow, and, as he went out of the shed, he felt the same sort of pinch at his ankles, which made him so angry that he kept striking with his whip in all directions, but hit nobody, for nobody was there.

But Jess—who, as soon as she heard the children's voices, had set up a most melancholy whinnying behind the locked stable door—began to neigh energetically. And Boxer barked, and the hens cackled, and the guinea fowls cried, "Come back, come back!" in their usual insane fashion—indeed the whole farmyard seemed in such an excited state that the children got frightened lest Gardener should scold them, and ran away, leaving Bill master of the field.

What an idle day he had! How he sat on the wall with his hands in his pockets, and lounged upon the fence, and sauntered round the garden! At length, absolutely tired of doing nothing, he went and talked with the Gardener's wife while she was hanging out her clothes. Gardener had gone down to the lower field, with all the little folks after him, so that he knew nothing of Bill's idling, or it might have come to an end.

By-and-by Bill thought it was time to go home to his supper. "But first I'll give Jess her corn," said he, "double quantity, and then I need not come back to give her her breakfast so early in the morning. Soh! you greedy beast. I'll be at you presently if you don't stop that noise."

For Jess, at sound of his footsteps, was heard to whinny in the most imploring manner, enough to have melted a heart of stone.

"The key—where on earth did I put the key?" cried Bill, whose constant habit it was to lay things out of his hand and then forget where he had put them, causing himself endless loss of time in searching for them—as now. At last he suddenly remembered the corner of the cow's manger, where he felt sure he had left it. But the key was not there.

"You can't have eaten it, you silly old cow," said he, striking Dolly on the nose as she rubbed herself against him—she was an affectionate beast. "Nor you, you stupid old hen!" kicking the mother of the brood, who with her fourteen chicks, being shut out of their usual roosting place, Jess's stable—kept pecking about under Dolly's legs. "It can't have gone without hands—of course it can't." But most certainly the key was gone.

What in the world should Bill do? Jess kept on making a pitiful complaining. No wonder, as she had not tasted food since morning. It would have made any kindhearted person quite sad to hear her, thinking how exceedingly hungry the poor pony must be.

Little did Bill care for that, or for anything, except that he should be sure to get into trouble as soon as he was found out. When he heard Gardener coming into the farmyard, with the children after him, Bill bolted over the wall like a flash of lightning, and ran away home, leaving poor Jess to her fate.

All the way he seemed to hear at his heels a little dog yelping, and then a swarm of gnats buzzing round his head, and altogether was so perplexed and bewildered that when he got into his mother's cottage he escaped into bed, and pulled the blanket over his ears to shut out the noise of the dog and the gnats, which at last turned into a sound like somebody laughing. It was not his mother, she didn't often laugh, poor soul!—Bill bothered her quite too much for that, and he knew it. Dreadfully frightened, he hid his head under the bedclothes, determined to go to sleep and think about nothing till next day.

Meantime, Gardener returned with all the little

people trooping after him. He had been rather kinder to them than usual this day, because he knew their mother had gone away in trouble, and now he let them help him to roll the gravel, and fetch up Dolly to be milked, and watch him milk her in the cowshed—where, it being nearly winter, she always spent the night now. They were so well amused that they forgot all about their disappointment as to the ride, and Jess did not remind them of it by her whinnying. For as soon as Bill was gone, she grew quite silent.

Brownie coaxed Jess into a deep stream

At last one little girl, the one who had cried over Jess's being left hungry, remembered the poor pony, and peeping through a crevice in the cowshed saw her stand contentedly munching at a large bowlful of corn.

"So Bill did find the key. I'm very glad," thought the kind little maiden, and to make sure looked again, when—what do you think she beheld squatting on the manger? Something brown, either a large brown rat, or a small brown man. But she held her tongue, since being a very little girl people sometimes laughed at her for the strange things she saw. She was quite certain she did see them for all that.

So she and the rest of the children went indoors and to bed. When they were fast asleep, something happened. Something so curious that the youngest boy, who, thinking he heard Jess neighing, got up to look out, was afraid to tell, lest he too should be laughed at, and went back to bed immediately.

In the middle of the night, a little old brown man, carrying a lantern, or at least having a light in his hand that looked like a lantern—went and unlocked Jess's stable, and patted her pretty head. At first she started, but soon she grew quiet and pleased, and let him do what he chose with her. He began rubbing her down, making the same funny hissing with his mouth that Bill did, and all grooms do—I never could find out why. But Jess evidently liked it, and stood as good as possible.

"Isn't it nice to be clean?" said the wee man, talking to her as if she were a human being, or a Brownie. "And I dare say your poor little legs ache with standing still so long. Shall we have a run together? The moon shines bright in the clear, cold night. Dear me! I'm talking poetry."

But Brownies are not poetical fairies, but quite commonplace, and up to all sorts of work. So, while he talked, he was saddling and bridling Jess, she not objecting in the least. Finally he jumped on her back.

" 'Off, said the stranger; off, off, and away!' " sang Brownie, mimicking a song of the Cook's. People in that house often heard their songs repeated in the oddest way, from room to room, everybody fancying it was somebody else that did it. But it was only the Brownie. "Now, 'A southerly wind and a cloudy sky proclaim it a hunting morning!' "

Or night—for it was the middle of the night, though bright as day—and Jess galloped and the Brownie sat on her back as merrily as if they had gone hunting together all their days.

Such a steeplechase it was! They cleared the farmyard at a single bound, and went flying down the road, and across the plowed field, and into the wood. Then out into the open country, and by-and-by into a dark, muddy lane—and oh! how muddy Devonshire lanes can be sometimes.

"Let's go into the water to wash ourselves," said Brownie, and coaxed Jess into a deep stream, which she swam as bravely as possible—she had not had such a frolic since she had left her native Shetland Isles. Up the bank she scrambled, her long hair dripping as if she had been a water dog instead of a pony. Brownie too shook himself like a rat or a beaver, throwing a shower round him in all directions.

"Never mind, at it again, my lass!" and he urged Jess into the water once more. Out she came, wetter and brisker than ever, and went back home through the lane, and the wood, and the plowed field, galloping like the wind, and tossing back her ears and mane and tail, perfectly frantic with enjoyment.

But when she reached her stable, the plight she was in would have driven any respectable groom frantic too. Her sides were white with foam, and the mud was sticking all over her like a plaster. As for her beautiful long hair, it was all caked together in a tangle, as if all the combs in the world would never make it smooth again. Her mane especially was plaited into knots, which people in Devonshire call elf locks, and say, when they find them on their horses, that it is because the fairies have been riding them.

Certainly, poor Jess had been pretty well ridden that night! When, just as the dawn began to break, Gardener got up and looked into the farmyard, his sharp eye caught sight of the stable door, wide open.

"Well done, Bill," shouted he, "up early at last. One hour before breakfast is worth three after."

But no Bill was there; only Jess, trembling and shaking, all in a foam, and muddy from head to foot, but looking perfectly cheerful in her mind. And out from under her forelegs ran a small creature, which Gardener mistook for Tiny, only Tiny was gray, and this dog was brown, of course!

I should not like to tell you all that was said to Bill, when, an hour after breakfast time, he came skulking up to the farm. In fact, words failing, Gardener took a good stick and laid it about Bill's shoulders, saying he would either do this, or tell the mistress of him, and how he had left the stable door open all night, and some bad fellow had stolen Jess, and galloped her all across the country, till, if she hadn't been the cleverest pony in the world, she never could have got back again.

Bill durst not contradict this explanation of the story. Especially as the key was found hanging up in its proper place by the kitchen door. And when he went to fetch it, he heard the most extraordinary sound in the coal cellar close by—like somebody snoring or laughing. Bill took to his heels, and did not come back for a whole hour.

But when he did come back, he made himself as busy as possible. He cleaned Jess, which was half a day's work at least. Then he took the little people to ride, and afterwards put his stable in the most beautiful order, and altogether was such a changed Bill that Gardener told him he must have left himself at home and brought back somebody else. Whether or not, the boy certainly improved, so that there was less occasion to find fault with him afterwards.

Jess lived to be quite an old pony, and carried a great many people—little people always, for she herself never grew any bigger. But I don't think she ever carried a Brownie again.

ADVENTURE
THE FIFTH

Brownie on the Ice

WINTER WAS a grand time for the six
little children, especially when they
had frost and snow. This happened
seldom enough for it to be the greatest
possible treat when it did happen; and it never
lasted very long, for the winters are warm in Devonshire.

There was a little lake three fields off, which made
the most splendid sliding place imaginable. No
skaters went near it, it was not large enough; and
besides, there was nobody to skate, the neighborhood being lonely. The lake itself looked the loneli-
est place imaginable. It was not very deep, not deep

enough to drown a man, but it had a gravelly bottom and was always very clear. Also the trees round
it grew so thick that they sheltered it completely
from the wind. So when it did freeze, it generally
froze as smooth as a sheet of glass.

"The lake bears!" was such a grand event, and so
rare, that, when it did occur, the news came at once
to the farm, and the children carried it as quickly to
their mother. For she had promised them that, if
such a thing did happen this year—it did not happen
every year—lessons should be stopped entirely, and
they should all go down to the lake and slide, if
they liked, all day long.

So, one morning just before Christmas, the eldest
boy ran in with a countenance of great delight.

"Mother, mother, the lake bears!" (It was rather
a compliment to call it a lake, it being only about
twenty yards across and forty long.) "The lake really
bears!"

"Who says so?"

"Bill. Bill has been on it for an hour this morning,
and has made us two such beautiful slides, he says—
an up-slide and a down-slide. May we go to them
directly?"

The mother hesitated.

"You promised, you know," pleaded the children.

"Very well, then; only be careful."

"And may we slide all day long, and never come home for dinner or anything?"

"Yes, if you like. Only Gardener must go with you, and stay all day."

This they did not like at all; nor when Gardener was spoken to, did he.

"You bothering children! I hope you may all get a good ducking in the lake! Serve you right for making me lose a day's work, just to look after you little monkeys. I've a great mind to tell your mother I won't do it."

But he did not, being fond of his mistress. He was also fond of his work, but he had no notion of play. I think the saying of "All work and no play makes Jack a dull boy" must have been applied to him, for Gardener, whatever he had been as a boy, was certainly a dull and melancholy man. The children used to say that if he and idle Bill could have been kneaded into one, and baked in the oven—a very warm oven—they would have come out rather a pleasant person.

As it was, Gardener was anything but a pleasant person, above all to spend a long day with—and on the ice, where one needs all one's cheerfulness and good humor to bear pinched fingers and numbed toes, and trips, and tumbles, and various uncomfortablenesses.

"He'll growl at us all day long—he'll be a regular spoil-sport!" lamented the children. "Oh! mother, mightn't we go alone?"

"No!" said the mother; and her "No" meant no, though she was always very kind. They argued the point no more, but started off, rather downhearted. But soon they regained their spirits, for it was a bright, clear, frosty day; the sun shining, though not enough to melt the ice, and just sufficient to lie like a thin sprinkling over the grass, and turn the brown branches into white ones. The little people danced along to keep themselves warm, carrying between them a basket which held their lunch. A very harmless lunch it was, just a large brown loaf and a lump of cheese and a knife to cut it with. Tossing the basket about in their fun, they managed to tumble the knife out, and were having a search for it in the long grass when Gardener came up, grumpily enough.

"To think of trusting you children with one of the table knives and a basket! What a fool Cook must be! I'll tell her so, and if they're lost she'll blame me. Give me the things."

He put the knife angrily in one pocket. "Perhaps it will cut a hole in it," said one of the children, in rather a pleased tone than otherwise. Then he turned the lunch all out on the grass and crammed it in the other pocket, hiding the basket behind a hedge.

"I'm sure I'll not be at the trouble of carrying it," said he, when the children cried out at this, "and you shan't carry it either, for you'll knock it about and spoil it. And as for your lunch getting warm in my pocket, why, so much the better this cold day."

It was not a lively joke, and they knew his pocket was very dirty. Indeed, the little girls had seen him stuff a dead rat into it only the day before. They looked ready to cry, but there was no help for them, except going back and complaining to their mother, and they did not like to do that. Besides, they knew that though Gardener was cross he was trustworthy, and she would never let them go down to the lake without him.

So they followed him, trying to be as good as they could—though it was difficult work. One of them proposed pelting him with snowballs, as they pelted each other. But at the first—which fell in his neck— he turned round so furiously that they never sent a second, but walked behind him as meek as mice.

As they went they heard little steps pattering after them.

"Perhaps it is the Brownie coming to play with us —I wish he would," whispered the youngest girl to the eldest boy, whose hand she generally held. And then the little pattering steps sounded again, traveling through the snow, but they saw nobody—so they said nothing.

The children would have liked to go straight to the ice: but Gardener insisted on taking them a mile round, to look at an extraordinary animal which a farmer there had just got—sent by his brother in Australia. The two old men stood gossiping so long that the children became extremely wearied. Every minute seemed an hour till they got on the ice.

At last one of them pulled Gardener's coattails, and whispered that they were quite ready to go.

"Then I'm not," and he waited ever so much longer, and got a drink of hot cider, which made him quite lively for a little while.

But by the time they reached the lake he was as cross as ever. He struck the ice with his stick, but made no attempt to see if it really did bear—though he would not allow the children to go one step upon it till he had tried.

"I know it doesn't bear, and you'll just have to go home again—a good thing, too—saves me from losing a day's work."

"Try, only try; Bill said it bore," implored the boys, and looked wistfully at the two beautiful slides —just as Bill said, one up and one down—stretching all the way across the lake; "of course it bears, or Bill could not have made these slides."

"Bill's an ass!" said the Gardener, and put his heavy foot cautiously on the ice. Just then there was seen jumping across it a creature which certainly had never been seen on ice before. It made the most extraordinary bounds on its long hind legs, with its little forelegs tucked up in front of it as if it wanted to carry a muff; and its stiff tail sticking out straight behind to balance itself with, apparently. The children at first started with surprise, and then burst out

laughing, for it was the funniest creature, and had the funniest way of getting along, that they had ever seen in their lives.

"It's the kangaroo!" cried Gardener in great excitement. "It has got loose—and it's sure to be lost—and what a way Mr. Giles will be in! I must go and tell him. Or stop, I'll try and catch it."

But in vain—it darted once or twice across the ice, dodging him, as it were; and once coming so close that he nearly caught it by the tail—to the children's great delight—then it vanished.

"I must go and tell Mr. Giles directly," said Gardener, and then stopped. For he had promised not to leave the children—and it was such a wild-goose chase after an escaped kangaroo. But he might get half-a-crown as a reward, and he was sure of another glass of cider.

"You just stop quiet here, and I'll be back in five minutes," said he to the children. "You may go a little way on the ice—I think it's sound enough. Only mind you don't tumble in, for there'll be nobody to pull you out."

"Oh, no," said the children, clapping their hands. They did not care for tumbling in, and were quite glad there was nobody there to pull them out. They hoped Gardener would stop a very long time away— only, as someone suggested when he was seen hurrying across the snowy field—he had taken away their lunch in his pocket, too.

"Never mind—we're not hungry yet. Now for a slide."

Off they darted, the three elder boys, with a good run. The biggest of the girls followed after them, and soon the whole four were skimming one after the other, as fast as a railway train, across the slip-

pery ice. And like a railway train, they had a colli-
sion, and all came tumbling one over the other, with
great screaming and laughter, to the high bank on
the other side.

The two younger ones were standing mournfully
watching the others from the opposite bank—when
suddenly there stood beside them a small brown
man.

"Ho-ho! little people," said he, coming between
them and taking hold of a hand of each. His was so
warm and theirs so cold that it was quite comfortable. And then somehow they found in their open
mouths a nice lozenge—I think it was peppermint,
but am not sure—which comforted them still more.

"Did you want me to play with you?" cried the
Brownie. "Then here I am! What shall we do? Have
a turn on the ice together?"

No sooner said than done. The two little children
felt themselves floating along—it was more like floating than running—with Brownie between them; up
the lake, and down the lake, and across the lake, not
at all interfering with the sliders—indeed, it was a
great deal better than sliding. Rosy and breathless,
their toes so nice and warm, and their hands feeling
like mince pies just taken out of the oven—the little
ones came to a standstill.

The elder ones stopped their sliding, and looked
toward Brownie with entreating eyes. He swung

himself up to a willow bough, and then turned head over heels onto the ice.

"Hallo, you don't mean to say you big ones want a race too. Well, come along—if the two eldest will give a slide to the little ones."

He watched them take a tiny sister between them, and slide her up one slide and down another, screaming with delight. Then he took the two middle children in either hand.

"One, two, three, and away!" Off they started—scudding along as light as feathers and as fast as steam engines over the smooth black ice, so clear that they could see the bits of stick and water grasses frozen in it, and even the little fishes swimming far down below—if they had only looked long enough.

When all had had their fair turns, they began to be frightfully hungry.

"Catch a fish for dinner, and I'll lend you a hook," said Brownie. At which they all laughed and then looked rather grave. Pulling a cold, raw, live fish from under the ice, and eating it was not a pleasant idea of dinner. "Well, what would you like to have? Let the little one choose."

She said, after thinking a minute, that she should like a currant cake.

"And I'd give you all a bit of it—a very large bit —I would indeed!" added she—almost with tears in her eyes—she was so very hungry.

"Do it then!" said the Brownie in his little squeaking voice.

Immediately the stone that the little girl was sitting on—a round hard stone and so cold!—turned into a nice hot cake—so hot that she jumped up directly. As soon as she saw what it was, she clapped her hands for joy.

"Oh, what a beautiful, beautiful cake! only we haven't got a knife to cut it."

The boys felt in all their pockets, but somehow their knives never were there when they were wanted.

"Look! you've got one in your hand!" said Brownie to the little one; and that minute a bit of stick she held turned into a bread knife—silver, with an ivory handle—big enough, and sharp enough, without being too sharp. For the youngest girl was not allowed to use sharp knives, though she liked cutting things indeed, especially cakes.

"That will do. Sit you down and carve the dinner. Fair shares, and don't let anybody eat too much. Now begin, ma'am," said the Brownie, quite politely, as if she had been ever so old.

Oh, how proud the little girl was! How bravely she set to work, and cut five of the biggest slices you ever saw, and gave them to her brothers and sisters,

and was just going to take the sixth slice for herself, when she remembered the Brownie.

"I beg your pardon," said she, as politely as he, though she was such a very little girl—and turned round to the wee brown man. But he was nowhere to be seen. The slices of cake in the children's hands remained cake, and uncommonly good it was, and such substantial eating that it did nearly the same as dinner. But the cake itself turned suddenly into a stone again, and the knife into a bit of stick.

For there was the Gardener, coming clumping along by the bank of the lake, and growling as he went.

"Have you got the kangaroo?" shouted the children, determined to be civil if possible.

"This place is bewitched, I think," said he. "The kangaroo was fast asleep in the cowshed. What! how dare you laugh at me?"

But they hadn't laughed at all. And they found it no laughing matter, poor children, when Gardener came on the ice, and began to scold them and order them about. He was perfectly savage with crossness, for the people at Giles's Farm had laughed at him very much, and he did not like to be laughed at— and at the top of the field he had by chance met his wife, and she had asked him severely how he could think of leaving the children alone.

Altogether his conscience pricked him a good deal; and when people's consciences prick them, sometimes they get angry with other people, which is very silly and only makes matters worse.

"What have you been doing all this time?" said he.

"All this five minutes?" said the eldest boy mischievously; for Gardener was only to be away five minutes, and he had stayed a full hour. Also, when

he fumbled in his pocket for the children's lunch—
to stop their tongues perhaps—he found it was not
there.

They set up a great outcry—for in spite of the
cake, they could have eaten a little more. Indeed, the
frost had such an effect upon all their appetites that
they felt not unlike that celebrated gentleman of
whom it is told that

> He ate a cow, and ate a calf,
> He ate an ox, and ate a half;
> He ate a church, he ate the steeple,
> He ate the priest, and all the people,
> And said he hadn't had enough then.

"We're so hungry, so very hungry. Couldn't you
go back again and fetch us some dinner?" cried they
entreatingly.

"Not I indeed. You may go back to dinner yourselves. You shall indeed, for I want my dinner too.
Two hours is plenty long enough to stop on the ice."

"It isn't two hours—it's only one."

"Well, one will do better than more. You're all
right now—and you might soon tumble in, or break
your legs on the slide. So come away home."

It wasn't kind of Gardener, and I don't wonder
the children felt it hard. Indeed, the eldest boy resisted stoutly.

"Mother said we might stop all day, and we will
stop all day. You may go home if you like."

"I won't, and you shall!" said Gardener, smacking a whip that he carried in his hand. "Stop till I catch you, and I'll give you this about your back, my fine gentleman."

And he tried to follow, but the little fellow darted across the ice—objecting to be either caught or whipped. It may have been rather naughty, but I am afraid it was great fun, dodging the Gardener up and down; he being too timid to go on the slippery ice, and sometimes getting so close that the whip nearly touched the lad.

"Bless us! there's the kangaroo again!" said he, starting. Just as he had caught the boy, and lifted the whip, the creature was seen hop-hopping from bank to bank. "I can't surely be mistaken this time. I must catch it."

Which seemed quite easy, for it limped as if it was lame, or as if the frost had bitten its toes, poor beast. Gardener went after it, walking cautiously on the slippery, crackling ice, and never minding whether or not he walked on the slides, though they called out to him that his nailed boots would spoil them.

But whether it was that ice which bears a boy will not bear a man, or whether, at each lame step of the kangaroo, there came a great crack, is more than I can tell. However, just as Gardener reached the middle of the lake, the ice suddenly broke and in he popped. The kangaroo too, apparently, for it was not seen afterwards.

What a hullabaloo the poor man made! Not that he was drowning—the lake was too shallow to drown anybody; but he got terribly wet, and the water was very cold. He soon scrambled out, the boys helping

him; and then he hobbled home as fast as he could, not even saying "Thank you" or taking the least notice of them.

Indeed, nobody took any notice of them—nobody came to fetch them, and they might have stayed sliding the whole afternoon. Only somehow they did not feel quite easy in their minds. And though the hole in the ice closed up immediately, and it seemed as firm as ever, still they did not like to slide upon it again.

"I think we had better go home and tell mother everything," said one of them. "Besides, we ought to see what has become of poor Gardener. He was very wet."

"Yes; but oh, how funny he looked!" And they all burst out laughing at the recollection of the figure he cut, scrambling out through the ice with his trousers dripping up to the knees, and the water running out of his boots, making a little pool wherever he stepped.

"And it freezes so hard that by the time he gets home his clothes will be as stiff as a board. His wife will have to put him to the fire to thaw before he can get out of them."

Again the little people burst into shouts of laughter. Although they laughed they were a little sorry for poor old Gardener, and hoped no great harm had come to him, but that he had got safely home and been dried by his own warm fire.

The frosty mist was beginning already to rise, and the sun, though still high up in the sky, looked like a ball of red-hot iron, as the six children went homeward across the fields—merry enough still, but not quite so merry as they had been a few hours before.

"Let's hope mother won't be vexed with us," said they, "but will let us come back again tomorrow. It wasn't our fault that Gardener tumbled in."

As somebody said this, they all heard quite distinctly, "Ha, ha, ha," and "Ho, ho, ho," and a sound of little steps pattering behind.

But whatever they thought, nobody ventured to say that it was the fault of the Brownie.

ADVENTURE
THE SIXTH

Brownie and the Clothes

ILL THE NEXT TIME: but when there is a Brownie in the house, no one can say that any of his tricks will be the last. For there's no stopping a Brownie, and no getting rid of him either. This one had followed the family from house to house, generation after generation—never any older, and sometimes seeming even to grow younger, by the tricks he played. In fact, though he looked like an old man, he was a perpetual child.

To the children he never did any harm; quite the contrary. And his chief misdoings were against those who vexed the children. But he gradually made friends with several of his grown-up enemies. Cook, for instance, who had ceased to be lazy at night and late in the morning, found no more black footmarks on her white tablecloth. And Brownie found his basin of milk waiting for him, night after night, behind the coal-cellar door.

Bill, too, got on well enough with his pony, and Jess was taken on no more night rides. No ducks were lost—and Dolly gave her milk quite comfortably to whoever milked her. Alas! this was either Bill or the Gardener's wife now. After that adventure on the ice, poor Gardener very seldom appeared. When he did, it was on two crutches, for he had had rheumatism in his feet, and could not stir outside his cottage door. Bill, therefore, had double work; which was probably all the better for Bill.

The garden had to take care of itself, but this being wintertime it did not much matter. Besides, Brownie seldom went into the garden, except in summer. During the hard weather he preferred to stop in his coal cellar. It might not have been a lively place, but it was warm, and he liked it.

He had company there too, for when the cat had more kittens—the kitten he used to tease being grown up now—they were all put in a hamper in the coal cellar; and of cold nights Brownie used to jump in beside them and be as warm and as cozy as a kitten himself. The little things never were heard to mew, so it may be supposed they liked his society. And the old mother cat evidently bore him no malice for the whipping she had got by mistake, so Brownie must have found means of coaxing her over. One thing you may be sure of, that all the while she and her kittens were in his coal cellar he took care never to turn himself into a mouse.

He was spending the winter on the whole very comfortably—without much trouble either to himself or his neighbors, when one day, the coal cellar being nearly empty, two men, and a great wagonload of coal behind them, came to the door, Gardener's wife following.

"My man says you're to give the cellar a good cleaning out before you put any more in," said she in her sharp voice; "and don't be lazy about it. It'll not take you ten minutes, for it's nearly all coal dust, except one big lump in the corner—you might clear that out too."

"Stop, it's the Brownie's lump! better not meddle with it," whispered the little scullery maid.

"Don't you meddle with matters that can't concern you," said the Gardener's wife, who had been thinking what a nice help it would be to her fire. To be sure, it was not her lump of coal, but she thought she might take it; the mistress would never miss it, nor the Brownie either. He must be a very silly old Brownie to live under a lump of coal.

So she argued with herself, and made the men lift it. "You must lift it, you see, if you are to sweep the coal cellar out clean. And you may as well put it on the barrow, and I'll wheel it out of your way."

This she said in quite a civil voice, lest they should tell of her, and stood by while it was being done. It was done without anything happening, except that a large rat ran out of the coal-cellar door, bouncing against her feet and frightening her so much that she nearly tumbled down.

"See what nonsense it is to talk of Brownies living in a coal cellar. Nothing lives there but rats, and I'll have them poisoned pretty soon, and get rid of them."

But she was rather frightened all the same, for the rat had been such a very big rat, and had looked at her as it darted past with such wild, bright, mischievous eyes—brown eyes, of course—that she all but jumped with surprise.

However, she had got her lump of coal, and was wheeling it quietly away, nobody seeing, to her cottage at the bottom of the garden. She was a hard-working woman—and her husband's illness made things even harder for her. Still she did not feel quite easy about taking what did not belong to her.

"I don't suppose anybody will miss the coal," she repeated. "I dare say the mistress would have given

it to me if I had asked her—and as for its being the
Brownie's lump—fudge! Bless us, what's that?"

For the barrow began to creak dreadfully, and
every creak sounded like the cry of a child, just as if

the wheel were going over its leg and crushing its
poor little bones.

"What a horrid noise! I must grease the barrow.
If only I knew where they keep the grease box. All

goes wrong now my old man's laid up. Oh, dear, Oh, dear!"

For suddenly the barrow had tilted over, though there was not a single stone near, and the big coal was tumbled onto the ground, where it broke into a thousand pieces. Gathering it up again was hopeless, and it made such a mess on the gravel walk that the old woman was thankful her misfortune happened behind the privet hedge, where nobody was likely to come.

"I'll take a broom and sweep it up tomorrow. Nobody goes near the orchard now, except me when I hang out the clothes; so I need say nothing about it to the old man or anybody. But ah! deary me, what a beautiful lot of coal I've lost!"

She stood and looked at it mournfully and then went into her cottage, where she found two or three of the little children keeping Gardener company. They did not dislike to do this now, for he was so much kinder than he used to be—so quiet and patient, though he suffered very much. And he had never once reproached them for what they always remembered—how it was ever since the day he was on the ice with them that he got the rheumatism.

So, one or other of them made a point of going to see him every day, and telling him all the funny things they could think of—indeed, it was a contest among them who should first make Gardener laugh.

They did not succeed in doing that exactly—but they managed to make him smile—and he was always gentle and grateful to them; so that they sometimes thought it was rather nice his being ill.

But his wife was not pleasant; she grumbled all day long, and snapped at him and his visitors; being especially snappish this day, because she had lost her big lump of coal.

"I can't have you children come bothering here," said she crossly; "I want to wring out my clothes, and hang them to dry. Be off with you."

"Let us stop a little, just to tell Gardener this one curious thing about Dolly and the pig."

"And then we'll help you to take your clothes to the orchard. We can carry your basket between us —we can indeed."

That was the last thing the woman wished; for she knew that the children would be sure to see the mess on the gravel walk—and they were such inquisitive children—they noticed everything. They would want to know all about it, and how the bits of coal came there. It was a very awkward position. But people who take other people's property often do find themselves in awkward positions.

"Thank you, young gentlemen," said she, quite politely, "but, indeed, the basket is too heavy for you. However, you may stop and gossip a little longer with my old man. He likes it."

And while they were shut up with Gardener in his bedroom, off she went, carrying the basket on her head, and hung her clothes carefully out, the big things on lines between the fruit trees, and the little things, such as stockings and pocket handkerchiefs, stuck on the gooseberry bushes, or spread upon the clean green grass.

"Such a fine day as it is! They'll dry directly," said she cheerfully to herself. "Plenty of sun, and not a breath of wind to blow them about. I'll leave them for an hour or two, and come and fetch them in before it grows dark. Then I shall get all my folding done by bedtime, and have a clear day for ironing tomorrow."

But when she did fetch them in, having bundled them all together in the dusk of the evening, never was such a sight as those clothes! They were all twisted in the oddest way, the stockings turned inside out, with the heels and toes tucked into the legs. The sleeves of the shirts were tied together in double knots, the pocket handkerchiefs made into round balls, so tight that if you had pelted a person with them they would have given very hard blows indeed. And the whole looked as if, instead of having lain quietly on the grass and bushes, they had been dragged through heaps of mud and then stamped upon, so that there was not a clean inch from end to end.

"What a horrid mess!" cried the Gardener's wife, who had been at first very angry, and then very frightened. "But I know what it is. That nasty Boxer has got loose again. It's he that has done it."

"Boxer wouldn't tie shirt sleeves in double knots or make balls of pocket handkerchiefs," Gardener was heard to answer solemnly.

"Then it's those horrid children; they are always up to some mischief or other—just let me catch them."

"You'd better not," said somebody in a voice exactly like Gardener's, though he himself declared he had not spoken a word. Indeed, he was fast asleep.

"Well, it's the most extraordinary thing I ever heard of," the Gardener's wife said—supposing she was talking to her husband all the time. But soon she held her tongue, for she found here and there among the clothes all sorts of queer marks—marks of fingers and toes and heels, not in mud at all but in coal dust, as black as black could be.

Now as the place where the big lump of coal had tumbled out of the barrow was fully fifty yards from the orchard, and as the coal could not come to the clothes, and the clothes could not go without hands, the only conclusion she could arrive at was—well, no particular conclusion at all.

It was too late that night to begin washing again.

Besides, she was extremely tired, and her husband woke up rather worse than usual, so she just bundled the clothes up anyhow in a corner, put the kitchen to rights, and went mournfully to bed.

Next morning she got up long before it was light, washed her clothes through all over again, and it being impossible to dry them by the fire, went out with them once more, and began spreading them out in their usual corner in a hopeless and melancholy manner. While she was at it the little folks came trooping around her. She didn't scold them this time, she was too low-spirited.

"No! my old man isn't any better, and I don't fancy he ever will be," said she, in answer to their questions. "And everything's going wrong with us— just listen!" And she told the trick which had been played her about the clothes.

The little people tried not to laugh, but it was so funny. And even now, the minute she had done hanging them out, there was something so droll in the way the clothes blew about, without any wind; the shirts hanging with their necks downwards, as if there was a man inside them; and the drawers standing stiffly astride on the gooseberry bushes, for all the world as if they held a pair of legs still. As for Gardener's nightcaps—long white cotton, with a tassel at the top—they were alarming to look at; just like a head stuck on the top of a pole.

The whole thing was so peculiar, and the old woman so comical in her despair, that the children, after trying hard to keep it in, at last broke into shouts of laughter. She turned furiously upon them.

"It was you who did it."

"No, indeed it wasn't!" said they, jumping away

to escape her blows. For she had got one of her clothes props, and was laying about her in the most reckless manner. However, she hurt nobody, and then she suddenly burst out, not laughing, but crying.

"It's a cruel thing, whoever has done it, to play such tricks on a poor old body like me, with a sick husband that she works hard for, and not a child to help her. But I don't care. I'll wash my clothes again, if it's twenty times over—and I'll hang them out again in the very place, just to make you all ashamed of yourselves."

Perhaps the little people were ashamed of themselves, though they really had not done the mischief. But they knew quite well who had done it, and more than once they were about to tell; only, they were afraid if they did so they should vex the Brownie so much that he would never come and play with them any more.

So they looked at one another without speaking, and when the Gardener's wife had emptied her basket and dried her eyes, they said to her very kindly:

"Perhaps no harm may come to your clothes this time. We'll sit and watch them till they are dry."

"Just as you like; I don't care. Them that hides can find, and them that plays tricks knows how to stop 'em."

It was not a civil speech, but then things were hard for the poor old woman. She had been awake nearly all night, and up washing at daybreak; her eyes were red with crying, and her steps weary and slow. The little children felt quite sorry for her, and instead of going to play sat watching the clothes as patiently as possible.

Nothing came near them. Sometimes, as before,

the things seemed to dance about without hands, and turn into odd shapes as if there were people inside them; but not a creature was seen, and not a sound was heard. And though there was neither wind nor sun, very soon all the linen was perfectly dry.

"Let us fetch one of mother's baskets, and fold all up as tidily as possible—that is, the girls can do it, it's their business—and we boys will carry it safe to Gardener's cottage."

So said they, not liking to say that they could not trust the basket out of their sight for fear of Brownie —whom, indeed, they were expecting to see peer round from every bush. They began to have a secret fear that he was rather a naughty Brownie, but then, as the eldest little girl whispered, "he was only a Brownie, and knew no better." They themselves were growing big children, who would be men and women sometime; when they hoped they would never do anything wrong. (Their parents hoped the same, but doubted it.)

In a serious and careful manner they folded up the clothes, and laid them one by one in the basket without any mischief, until just as the two biggest boys were lifting their burden to carry it away, they felt something tugging at it from underneath.

"Hallo! Where are you taking all this rubbish? Better give it to me."

"No, if you please," said they very civilly, not to offend the little brown man. "We'll not trouble you, thanks! We'd rather do it ourselves. For poor old Gardener is very ill, and his wife is very miserable, and we are extremely sorry for them both."

"Extremely sorry!" cried Brownie, throwing up his cap in the air, and tumbling head over heels in an excited manner. "What in the world does extremely sorry mean?"

The children could not explain, especially to a Brownie, but they thought they understood—anyhow they felt it. And they looked so sorrowful that the Brownie could not tell what to make of it.

He could not be said to be sorry, since, being a Brownie and not a human being knowing right from wrong, he never tried particularly to do right and had no idea when he was doing wrong. But he seemed to have an idea he was troubling the children, and he never liked to see them look unhappy.

So he turned head over heels six times running and then came back again.

"The silly old woman! I washed her clothes for her last night in a way she didn't expect. I hadn't any soap, so I used a little mud and coal dust, and very pretty they looked. Ha, ha, ha! Shall I wash them over again tonight?"

"Oh, no, please don't!" implored the children.

"Shall I starch and iron them? I'll do it beauti-

fully. One—two—three, five—six—seven, Abracadabra, tum tum ti!" shouted he, jabbering all sorts
of nonsense, as it seemed to the children, and playing such antics that they stood and stared in the
utmost amazement, and quite forgot the clothes.
When they looked round again, the basket was
gone.

"Seek till you find, seek till you find,
  Under the biggest gooseberry bush, exactly to your
  mind."

They heard him singing this remarkable rhyme
long after they had lost sight of him. And then they
all set about searching. But it was a long while before they found, and still longer before they could
decide, which was the biggest gooseberry bush,
each child having his or her opinion—sometimes a
very strong one—on the matter. At last they agreed
to settle it by pulling half a dozen little sticks, to see
which stick was the longest, and the child that held
it was to decide the gooseberry bush.

This done, underneath the branches what should
they find but the identical basket of clothes! Only, instead of being roughly dried, they were all starched
and ironed in the most beautiful manner. As for
the shirts, they really were a picture to behold, and
the stockings were all folded up and even darned
in one or two places as neatly as possible. And

strange to tell, there was not a single black mark of feet or fingers on any one of them.

"Kind little Brownie! clever little Brownie!" cried the children in chorus, and thought this was the most astonishing trick he had ever played.

What the Gardener's wife said about it, whether they told her anything, or allowed her to suppose that the clothes had been done in their own laundry instead of the Brownie's (wherever that establishment might be), is more than I can tell. Of one thing only I am certain—that the little people said nothing but what was true. Also that the very minute they got home they told their mother everything.

But for a long time after that they were a good deal troubled. Gardener got better, and went hobbling about the place again, to his own and everybody's great content, and his wife was less sharptongued and complaining than usual—indeed, she had nothing to complain of. All the family were very flourishing—except the little Brownie.

Often there was heard a curious sound all over the house; it might have been rats squeaking behind the wainscot—the elders said it was—but the children were sure it was a sort of weeping and wailing.

> "They've stolen my coal,
> And I haven't a hole
> To hide in;

> Not even a house
> One could ask a mouse
> To bide in."

A most forlorn tune it was, ending in a dreary minor key, and it lasted for months and months—at least the children said it did. And they were growing quite dull for want of a playfellow, when, by the greatest good luck in the world, there came to the house, not only a new lot of kittens, but a new baby. And the new baby was everybody's pet—including the Brownie's.

From that time, though he was not often seen, he was continually heard up and down the staircase, where he was frequently mistaken for Tiny or the cat, and sent sharply down again, which was wasting a great deal of wholesome anger upon Mr. Nobody. Or he lurked in odd corners of the nursery, whither the baby was seen crawling eagerly after nothing in particular, or else she sat laughing with all her might at something—probably her own toes.

But as Brownie was never seen, he was never suspected. And since he did no mischief, neither pinched the baby nor broke the toys, left no soap in the bath and no footmarks about the room, but was always a well-conducted Brownie in every way, he was allowed to inhabit the nursery (or supposed to do so, since as nobody saw him nobody could prevent him), until the children were grown up into men and women.

After that he retired into his coal cellar, and for all I know he may live there still, and have gone through hundreds of adventures since—but as I never heard them I can't tell them. Only I think if I could be a little child again I should exceedingly like a Brownie to play with me. Should not you?

THE
INVISIBLE
PRINCE

THE

INVISIBLE PRINCE

THERE WERE A KING AND QUEEN who were dotingly fond of their only son, notwithstanding that he was equally deformed in mind and person. The King was quite sensible of the evil disposition of his son, but the Queen in her excessive fondness saw no fault whatever in her dear Furibon, as he was named. The surest way to win her favor was to praise Furibon for charms he did not possess. When he became of age to have a governor, the King made choice of a prince who had an ancient right to the crown, but was not able to support it. This Prince had a son, named Leander, handsome, accomplished, amiable—in every respect the opposite of Prince Furibon. The two were frequently together, which only made the deformed Prince more repulsive.

One day, certain ambassadors having arrived from a far country, the Prince stood in a gallery to see them. When, taking Leander for the King's son, they made their obeisance to him, treating Furibon as a mere dwarf, the latter was so offended that he drew his sword, and would have done them a mischief had not the King just then appeared. As it was, the affair produced a quarrel, which ended in Leander's being sent to a faraway castle belonging to his father.

There, however, he was quite happy, for he was a great lover of hunting, fishing, and walking. He understood painting, read much, and played upon several instruments, so that he was glad to be freed from the fantastic humors of Furibon. One day as he was walking in the garden, finding the heat intense, he retired into a shady grove and began to play upon the flute to amuse himself. As he played, he felt something wind about his leg, and looking down saw a great adder. He took his handkerchief, and catching it by the head was going to kill it. But the adder, looking steadfastly in his face, seemed to beg his pardon. At this instant one of the gardeners happened to come to the place where Leander was, and spying the snake, cried out to his master: "Hold it fast, sir; it is but an hour since we ran after it to kill it. It is the most mischievous creature in the world."

Leander, casting his eyes a second time upon the snake, which was speckled with a thousand extraordinary colors, perceived the poor creature still looked upon him with an aspect that seemed to implore compassion, and never tried in the least to defend itself.

"Though thou hast such a mind to kill it," said he to the gardener, "yet, as it came to me for refuge, I forbid thee to do it any harm. I will keep it, and when it has cast its beautiful skin I will let it go." He then returned home, and carrying the snake with him, put it into a large chamber, the key of which he kept himself, and ordered bran, milk, and flowers to be given to it, for its delight and sustenance; so that never was snake so happy. Leander went sometimes to see it, and when it perceived him it made haste to meet him, showing him all the little marks of love and gratitude of which a poor snake was capable, which did not a little surprise him, though he took no further notice of it.

In the meantime all the court ladies were extremely troubled at his absence, and he was the subject of all their discourse. "Alas!" cried they, "there is no pleasure at court since Leander is gone, of whose absence the wicked Furibon is the cause!" Furibon also had his parasites, for his power over the Queen made him feared. They told him what the ladies said, which enraged him to such a degree that in his passion he flew to the Queen's chamber, and vowed he would kill himself before her face if she did not find means to destroy Leander. The Queen, who also hated Leander, because he was handsomer than her son, replied that she had long looked upon him as a traitor, and therefore would willingly consent to his death. To which purpose she advised Furibon to go a-hunting with some of his confidants, and contrive it so that Leander should make one of the party.

"Then," said she, "you may find some way to punish him for pleasing everybody."

Furibon understood her, and accordingly went
a-hunting. And Leander, when he heard the horns
and the hounds, mounted his horse and rode to see
who it was. But he was surprised to meet the Prince
so unexpectedly. He alighted immediately and sa-
luted him with respect; and Furibon received him
more graciously than usual and bade him follow him.
All of a sudden he turned his horse and rode another
way, making a sign to the ruffians to take the first
opportunity to kill Leander. But before he had got
quite out of sight, a lion of prodigious size, coming
out of his den, leaped upon Furibon. All his follow-
ers fled, and only Leander remained; who, attacking
the animal sword in hand, by his valor and agility
saved the life of his most cruel enemy, who meanwhile had fallen in a swoon from fear.

When he recovered, Leander presented him his
horse to remount. Now, any other than such a wretch
would have been grateful, but Furibon did not even
look upon him. Nay, mounting the horse, he rode
in quest of the ruffians, to whom he repeated his
orders to kill his rescuer. They accordingly surrounded Leander, who, setting his back to a tree,
behaved with so much bravery that he laid them all
dead at his feet. Furibon, believing him by this time

slain, rode eagerly up to the spot. When Leander saw him he advanced to meet him. "Sir," said he, "if it was by your order that these assassins came to kill me, I am sorry I made any defense."

"You are an insolent villain!" replied Furibon, "and if ever you come into my presence again, you shall surely die."

Leander made no answer, but retired sad and pensive to his own home, where he spent the night in pondering what was best for him to do; for there was no likelihood he should be able to defend himself against the power of the King's son. Therefore he at length concluded he would travel abroad and see the world. Being ready to depart, he recollected his snake, and, calling for some milk and fruits, carried them to the poor creature for the last time. On opening the door he perceived an extraordinary luster in one corner of the room, and casting his eye on the place he was surprised to see a lady, whose noble and majestic air made him immediately conclude she was a princess of royal birth. Her habit was of purple satin, embroidered with pearls and diamonds. She advanced toward him with a gracious smile.

"Young Prince," said she, "you find no longer your pet snake, but me, the fairy Gentilla, ready to requite your generosity. For know that we fairies live a hundred years in flourishing youth, without diseases, without trouble or pain; and this term being expired, we become snakes for eight days. During that time it is not in our power to prevent any misfortune that may befall us; and if we happen to be killed, we never revive again. But these eight days being expired, we resume our usual form and recover our beauty, our power, and our riches. Now you know how much I am obliged to your goodness, and it is but just that I should repay my debt of gratitude. Think how I can serve you and depend on me."

The young Prince, who had never conversed with a fairy till now, was so surprised that it was a long time before he could speak. But at length, making a profound reverence, "Madam," said he, "since I have had the honor to serve you, I know not any other happiness that I can wish for."

"I should be sorry," replied she, "not to be of service to you in something. Consider, it is in my power to bestow on you long life, kingdoms, riches; to give you mines of diamonds and houses full of gold. I can make you an excellent orator, poet, musician, and painter; or, if you desire it, a spirit of the air, the water, or the earth."

Here Leander interrupted her. "Permit me, madam," said he, "to ask you what benefit it would be to me to be a spirit?"

"Much," replied the fairy, "you would be invisible

when you pleased, and might in an instant traverse the whole earth. You would be able to fly without wings, to descend into the abyss of the earth without dying, and walk at the bottom of the sea without being drowned. Nor doors, nor windows, though fast shut and locked, could hinder you from entering anywhere; and whenever you had a mind, you might resume your natural form."

"Oh, madam!" cried Leander, "then let me be a spirit. I am going to travel, and should prefer it above all those other advantages you have so generously offered me."

Gentilla thereupon stroking his face three times, "Be a spirit," said she; and then, embracing him, she gave him a little red cap with a plume of feathers. "When you put on this cap you shall be invisible; but when you take it off you shall again become visible."

Leander, overjoyed, put his little red cap upon his head and wished himself in the forest, that he might gather some wild roses which he had observed there. His body immediately became as light as thought. He flew through the window like a bird; though, in flying over the river, he was not without fear lest he should fall into it, and the power of the fairy not be able to save him. But he arrived in safety at the rosebushes, plucked the three roses, and returned immediately to his chamber. He presented

"When you put on this cap you shall be invisible..."

his roses to the fairy, overjoyed that his first experiments had succeeded so well. She bade him keep the roses, for one of them would supply him with money whenever he wanted it. If he put the other into his mistress's bosom, he would know whether she was faithful or not; and the third would keep him always in good health. Then, without staying to receive his thanks, she wished him success in his travels and disappeared.

Leander, infinitely pleased, settled his affairs, mounted the finest horse in the stable, called Gris-de-line, and attended by some of his servants in livery, made his return to court. Now you must know Furibon had given out that had it not been for his courage Leander would have murdered him when they were a-hunting. So the King, being importuned by the Queen, gave orders that Leander should be apprehended. But when he came, he showed so much courage and resolution that Furibon ran to the Queen's chamber and prayed her to order him to be seized. The Queen, who was extremely diligent in everything that her son desired, went immediately to the King.

Furibon, being impatient to know what would be resolved, followed her; but stopped at the door and laid his ear to the keyhole, putting his hair aside that he might the better hear what was said. At the same time, Leander entered the court-hall of the palace with his red cap upon his head. Perceiving Furibon listening at the door of the King's chamber, he took a nail and a hammer and nailed his ear to the door. Furibon began to roar, so that the Queen, hearing her son's voice, ran and opened the door, and, pulling it hastily, tore her son's ear from his head. Half out of her wits, she set him in her lap, took up his ear, kissed it, and clapped it again upon its place. But the invisible Leander, seizing upon a handful of twigs, with which they corrected the King's little dogs, gave the Queen several lashes upon her hands, and her son as many on the nose. Thereupon the Queen cried out, "Murder! murder!" and the King looked about, and the people came running in; but nothing was to be seen.

Some cried that the Queen was mad, and that her madness proceeded from her grief that her son had lost one ear. The King was as ready as any to believe it, so that when she came near him he avoided her, which made a very ridiculous scene.

Leander, then leaving the chamber, went into the garden, and there, assuming his own shape, he boldly began to pluck the Queen's cherries, apricots, strawberries, and flowers, though he knew she set such a high value on them that it was as much as a man's life was worth to touch one. The gardeners, all amazed, came and told their Majesties that Prince

Leander was making havoc of all the fruits and flowers in the Queen's garden.

"What insolence!" said the Queen. Then turning to Furibon, she said, "My pretty child, forget the pain of thy ear but for a moment, and fetch that vile wretch hither. Take our guards, both horse and foot, seize him, and punish him as he deserves."

Furibon, encouraged by his mother, and attended by a great number of armed soldiers, entered the garden and saw Leander; who, taking refuge under a tree, pelted them all with oranges. But when they came running toward him, thinking to have seized him, he was not to be seen. He had slipped behind Furibon, who was in a bad condition already. But Leander played him one trick more; for he pushed him down upon the gravel walk, and frightened him so that the soldiers had to take him up, carry him away, and put him to bed.

Satisfied with this revenge, he returned to his servants, who waited for him, and giving them money, sent them back to his castle, that none might know the secret of his red cap and roses. As yet he had not determined whither to go. However, he mounted his fine horse Gris-de-line, and, laying the reins upon his neck, let him take his own road. At length he arrived in a forest, where he stopped to shelter himself from the heat. He had not been

above a minute there before he heard a lamentable
noise of sighing and sobbing. Looking about him,
he beheld a man, who ran, stopped, then ran again,
sometimes crying, sometimes silent, then tearing his
hair, then thumping his breast like some unfortunate
madman. Yet he seemed to be both handsome and
young. His garments had been magnificent, but he
had torn them all to tatters. The Prince, moved with
compassion, made toward him, and mildly accosted
him. "Sir," said he, "your condition appears so deplorable that I must ask the cause of your sorrow,
assuring you of every assistance in my power."

"Oh, sir," answered the young man, "nothing can
cure my grief. This day my dear mistress is to be
sacrificed to a rich old ruffian of a husband who will
make her miserable."

"Does she love you, then?" asked Leander.

"I flatter myself so," answered the young man.

"Where is she?" continued Leander.

"In the castle at the end of this forest," replied
the lover.

"Very well," said Leander; "stay you here till I
come again, and in a little while I will bring you
good news."

He then put on his little red cap and wished himself in the castle. He had hardly arrived when he
heard all sorts of music. He entered into a great
room, where the friends and kindred of the old man

and the young lady were assembled. No one could look more amiable than she. But the paleness of her complexion, the melancholy that appeared in her countenance, and the tears that now and then dropped, as it were by stealth, from her eyes, betrayed the trouble of her mind.

Leander now became invisible, and placed himself in a corner of the room. He soon perceived the father and mother of the bride; and coming behind the mother's chair, whispered in her ear, "If you marry your daughter to that old dotard, before eight days are over you shall certainly die." The woman, frightened to hear such a terrible sentence pronounced upon her, and yet not knowing from whence it came, gave a loud shriek and dropped upon the floor. Her husband asked what ailed her. She cried that she was a dead woman if the marriage of her daughter went forward, and therefore she would not consent to it for all the world. Her husband laughed at her and called her a fool.

But the invisible Leander, accosting the man, threatened him in the same way, which frightened him so terribly that he also insisted on the marriage being broken off. When the lover complained, Leander trod hard upon his gouty toes and rang such an alarm in his ears that, not being able any longer to hear himself speak, away he limped, glad enough to go. The real lover soon appeared, and he and his fair mistress fell joyfully into each other's arms, the parents consenting to their union. Leander, assuming his own shape, appeared at the hall door, as if he were a stranger drawn thither by the report of this extraordinary wedding.

From hence he traveled on, and came to a great city, where, upon his arrival, he learned there was to be a great and solemn procession, to accompany a young woman against her will to be shut up among the vestal nuns. The Prince was touched with compassion. And thinking the best use he could make of his cap was to redress public wrongs and relieve the oppressed, he flew to the temple, where he saw the young woman, crowned with flowers, clad in white, and with her disheveled hair flowing about her shoulders. Two of her brothers led her by each hand, and her mother followed her with a great crowd of men and women.

Leander, being invisible, cried out, "Stop, stop, wicked brethren. Stop, rash and inconsiderate mother; if you proceed any farther, you shall be squeezed to death like so many frogs." They looked about, but could not conceive from whence these terrible threats came. The brothers said it was only their sister's lover, who had hid himself in some hole. Thereupon Leander, in wrath, took a long cudgel, and they had no reason to say the blows were not well laid on. The multitude fled, the vestals ran

away, and Leander was left alone with the victim.
Immediately he pulled off his red cap and asked her
wherein he might serve her. She answered him that
there was a certain gentleman whom she would be
glad to marry, but that he lacked an estate. Leander
then shook his rose so long that he supplied them

with a sackful of gold pieces; after which they were
married and lived happily together.

But his last adventure was the most agreeable of
all. Entering into a wide forest, he heard lamentable
cries. He looked about him in every direction and at
length he spied four men well armed, who were
carrying away by force a young lady, thirteen or
fourteen years of age. The Prince hastened forward

and accosted them. "What harm has this girl done?" said he.

"Ha! ha! my little master," cried he who seemed to be the ringleader of the rest, "who bade you inquire?"

"Let her alone," said Leander, "and go about your business."

"Oh, yes, to be sure," cried they, laughing; whereupon the Prince, alighting, put on his red cap, not thinking it otherwise prudent to attack four who seemed strong enough to fight a dozen. One of them stayed to take care of the young lady, while the three others went after Gris-de-line, who gave them a great deal of unwelcome exercise.

Meantime the young lady continued her cries and complaints. "Oh, my dear Princess," said she, "how happy was I in your palace! Did you but know my sad misfortune, you would send your Amazons to rescue poor Abricotina."

Leander, having listened to what she said, without delay seized the ruffian that held her, and bound him fast to a tree before he had time or strength to defend himself. He then went to the second, and taking him by both arms, bound him in the same manner to another tree. In the meantime Abricotina made the best of her good fortune and betook herself to her heels, not knowing which way she went. But Leander, missing her, called out to his horse

Gris-de-line; who, by two kicks with his hoof, rid himself of the two ruffians who had pursued him. One of them had his head broken and the other three of his ribs.

And now Leander wanted only to overtake Abricotina; for he thought her so handsome that he wished to see her again. He found her leaning against a tree. When she saw Gris-de-line coming toward her, "How lucky am I!" cried she; "this pretty little horse will carry me to the palace of pleasure." Leander heard her, though she saw him not. He rode up to her, brought Gris-de-line to a halt, and when Abricotina mounted him, Leander clasped her in his arms and placed her gently before him. Oh, how great was Abricotina's fear to feel herself fast embraced, and yet see nobody! She durst not stir, and shut her eyes for fear of seeing a spirit. But Leander took off his little cap. "How comes it, fair Abricotina," said he, "that you are afraid of me, who delivered you out of the hands of the ruffians?"

With that she opened her eyes, and knowing him again, "Oh, sir," said she, "I am infinitely obliged to you; but I was afraid, for I felt myself held fast and could see no one."

"Surely," replied Leander, "the danger you have been in has disturbed you and cast a mist before your eyes."

Abricotina would not seem to doubt him, though

she was otherwise extremely sensible. And after they had talked for some time of indifferent things, Lean-- der requested her to tell him her age, her country, and by what accident she had fallen into the hands of the ruffians.

"Know then, sir," said she, "there was a certain very great fairy married to a prince who wearied of her. She therefore banished him from her pres- ence, and established herself and daughter in the Island of Calm Delights. The Princess, who is my mistress, being very fair, has many lovers—among others, one named Furibon, whom she detests. He it was whose ruffians seized me today when I was wandering in search of a stray parrot. Accept, noble Prince, my best thanks for your valor, which I shall never forget."

Leander said how happy he was to have served her, and asked if he could not obtain admission into the island. Abricotina assured him this was impos- sible, and therefore he had better forget all about it. While they were thus conversing, they came to the bank of a large river. Abricotina alighted with a nimble jump from the horse.

"Farewell, sir," said she to the Prince, making a profound reverence; "I wish you every happiness."

"And I," said Leander, "wish that I may now and then have a small share in your remembrance."

So saying, he galloped away and soon entered

into the thickest part of the wood, near a river, where he unbridled and unsaddled Gris-de-line. Then, putting on his little cap, he wished himself in the Island of Calm Delights, and his wish was immediately accomplished.

The palace was of pure gold, and stood upon pillars of crystal and precious stones, which repre-

sented the zodiac and all the wonders of nature; all the arts and sciences; the sea, with all the variety of fish therein contained; the earth, with all the various creatures which it produces; the chases of Diana and her nymphs; the noble exercises of the Amazons; the amusements of a country life; flocks of sheep with their shepherds and dogs; the toils of agriculture, harvesting, gardening. And among all this variety of representations there was neither man nor boy to be seen—not so much as a little winged

Cupid; so highly had the Princess been incensed
against her inconstant husband as not to show the
least favor to his fickle sex.

"Abricotina did not deceive me," said Leander to
himself; "they have banished from hence the very
idea of men. Now let us see what they have lost by
it." With that he entered into the palace, and at
every step he took he met with objects so wonderful
that when he had once fixed his eyes upon them he
had much ado to take them off again. He viewed a
vast number of these apartments, some full of china,
no less fine than curious; others lined with porcelain,
so delicate that the walls were quite transparent.
Coral, jasper, agates, and cornelians adorned the
rooms of state, and the presence chamber was one
entire mirror. The throne was one great pearl, hol-
lowed like a shell. The Princess sat, surrounded by
her maidens, none of whom could compare with herself in loveliness. In her was all the innocent sweet-
ness of youth, combined with the dignity of matur-
ity. In truth, she was perfection; and so thought the
invisible Leander.

Not seeing Abricotina, the Princess asked where
she was. Thereupon Leander, being very desirous
to speak, assumed the tone of a parrot, for there
were many in the room, and addressed himself invisibly to the Princess.

"Most charming Princess," said he, "Abricotina

At first the Princess took Leander for a real statue

will return immediately. She was in great danger of being carried away from this place but for a young prince who rescued her."

The Princess was surprised by the parrot, his answer being so extremely pertinent.

"You are very rude, little parrot," said the Princess; "and Abricotina, when she comes, shall chastise you for it."

"I shall not be chastised," answered Leander, still counterfeiting the parrot's voice. "Moreover, she will let you know of the great desire that stranger had to be admitted into this palace, that he might convince you of the falsehood of those ideas which you have conceived against his sex."

"In truth, pretty parrot," cried the Princess, "it is a pity you are not every day so diverting; I should love you dearly."

"Ah! if prattling will please you, Princess," replied Leander, "I will prate from morning till night."

"But," continued the Princess, "how shall I be sure my parrot is not a sorcerer?"

"He is more in love than any sorcerer can be," replied the Prince.

At this moment Abricotina entered the room, and falling at her lovely mistress's feet, gave her a full account of what had befallen her, and described the Prince in the most glowing colors.

"I should have hated all men," added she, "had I

not seen him! Oh, madam, how charming he is! His air and all his behavior have something in them so noble. And though whatever he spoke was infinitely pleasing, yet I think I did well in not bringing him hither."

To this the Princess said nothing, but she asked Abricotina a hundred other questions concerning the Prince; whether she knew his name, his country, his birth, from whence he came, and whither he was going. And after this she fell into a profound reverie.

Leander observed everything, and continued to chatter as he had begun.

"Abricotina is ungrateful, madam," said he; "that poor stranger will die of grief if he sees you not."

"Well, parrot, let him die," answered the Princess with a sigh. "And since thou undertakest to reason like a person of wit, and not a little bird, I forbid thee to talk to me any more of this unknown person."

Leander was overjoyed to find that Abricotina and the parrot's discourse had made such an impression on the Princess. He looked upon her with pleasure and delight. "Can it be," said he to himself, "that the masterpiece of nature, that the wonder of our age, should be confined eternally on an island, and no mortal dare to approach her? But," continued he, "wherefore am I concerned that others are banished hence, since I have the happiness to be with her, to

hear and to admire her; nay, more, to love her above
all the women in the universe?"

It was late, and the Princess retired into a large
room of marble and porphyry, where several bub-
bling fountains refreshed the air with an agreeable
coolness. As soon as she entered the music began, a
sumptuous supper was served up, and the birds from
several aviaries on each side of the room, of which
Abricotina had the chief care, opened their little
throats in the most agreeable manner.

Leander had traveled a journey long enough to
give him a good appetite, which made him draw
near the table, where the very smell of such viands
was agreeable and refreshing. The Princess had a
curious tabby cat, for which she had a great kindness. This cat one of the maids of honor held in her
arms, saying, "Madam, Bluet is hungry!" With that
a chair was presently brought for the cat; for he was
a cat of quality, and had a necklace of pearl about
his neck. He was served on a golden plate with a
laced napkin before him; and the plate being supplied with meat, Bluet sat with the solemn importance of an alderman.

"Ho! ho!" cried Leander to himself; "an idle tabby
malkin, that perhaps never caught a mouse in his
life, and I dare say is not descended from a better
family than myself, has the honor to sit at table with

my mistress. I would fain know whether he loves her so well as I do."

Saying this, he placed himself in the chair with the cat upon his knee, for nobody saw him, because he had his little red cap on. Finding Bluet's plate well supplied with partridge, quail, and pheasant, he made so free with them that whatever was set before Master Puss disappeared in a trice. The whole

court said no cat ever ate with a better appetite. There were excellent ragouts, and the Prince made use of the cat's paw to taste them. But he sometimes pulled his paw too roughly, and Bluet, not understanding raillery, began to mew and be quite out of patience. The Princess observing it, "Bring that fricassee and that tart to poor Bluet," said she; "see how he cries to have them."

Leander laughed to himself at the pleasantness of this adventure. But he was very thirsty, not being accustomed to partake of such bountiful repasts without something to drink. By the help of the cat's paw he got a melon, with which he somewhat quenched his thirst; and when supper was quite over, he went to the buffet and took two bottles of delicious wine.

The Princess now retired into her boudoir, ordering Abricotina to follow her and make fast the door. But they could not keep out Leander, who was there as soon as they. However, the Princess, believing herself alone with her confidante, said:

"Abricotina, tell me truly, did you exaggerate in your description of the unknown Prince, for methinks it is impossible he should be as amiable as you say?"

"Madam," replied the damsel, "if I have failed in anything, it was in coming short of what was due to him."

The Princess sighed and was silent for a time; then resuming her speech, "I am glad," said she, "thou didst not bring him with thee."

"But, madam," answered Abricotina, who was a cunning girl, and already had penetrated her mistress's thoughts, "suppose he had come to admire the wonders of these beautiful mansions, what harm could he have done us? Will you live eternally unknown in a corner of the world, concealed from the rest of human kind? Of what use is all your grandeur, pomp, magnificence, if nobody sees it?"

"Hold thy peace, prattler," replied the Princess, "and do not disturb that happy repose which I have enjoyed so long."

Abricotina durst make no reply. And the Princess, having awaited her answer for some time, asked her whether she had anything to say. Abricotina then said she thought it was to very little purpose that her mistress had sent her picture to the courts of several princes, since it only served to make those who saw it miserable; that everyone would be desirous to marry her, and as she could not marry them all, indeed none of them, it would make them desperate.

"Yet, for all that," said the Princess, "I could wish my picture were in the hands of this same stranger."

"Oh, madam," answered Abricotina, "is not his desire to see you violent enough already? Would you augment it?"

"Yes," cried the Princess; "a certain impulse of vanity, which I was never sensible of till now, has bred this foolish fancy in me."

Leander heard all this discourse, and lost not a tittle of what she said. Some of her expressions gave him hope, others absolutely destroyed it. The Princess presently asked Abricotina whether she had seen anything extraordinary during her short travels.

"Madam," said she, "I passed through one forest where I saw certain creatures that resembled little children. They skip and dance upon the trees like squirrels; they are very ugly, but have wonderful agility and address."

"I wish I had one of them," said the Princess. "But if they are so nimble as you say they are, it is impossible to catch one."

Leander, who had passed through the same forest, knew what Abricotina meant, and presently wished himself in the place. He caught a dozen little monkeys, some bigger, some less, and all of different colors, and with much ado put them into a large sack. Then, wishing himself in Paris, where, he had heard, a man might have everything for money, he went and bought a little gold chariot. He taught six green monkeys to draw it. They were harnessed with fine traces of flame-colored morocco leather. He went to another place, where he met with two monkeys of merit, the more pleasant of which was called Briscambril, the other Pierceforest—both very spruce and well educated. He dressed Briscambril like a king and placed him in the coach. Pierceforest he made the coachman. The others were dressed like pages. All these he put into his sack, coach and all.

The Princess not yet having gone to bed, heard a rumbling of a little coach in the long gallery. At the same time, her ladies came to tell her that the king of the dwarfs was arrived, and the chariot immediately entered her chamber with all the monkey train. The country monkeys began to show a thousand tricks, which far surpassed those of Briscambril and Pierceforest. To say the truth, Leander conducted the whole performance. He drew the chariot where Briscambril sat arrayed as a king, and making him hold a box of diamonds in his hand, he presented it with a becoming grace to the Princess. The Princess' surprise may be easily imagined. Moreover, Briscambril made a sign for Pierceforest to come and dance with him. The most celebrated dancers were not to be compared with them in activity. But the Princess, troubled that she could not guess from whence this curious present came, dismissed the dancers sooner than she would otherwise have done, though she was extremely pleased with them.

Leander, satisfied with having seen the delight the Princess had taken in beholding the monkeys, thought of nothing now but to get a little repose, which he greatly needed. He stayed some time in the great gallery; afterward, going down a pair of stairs, and finding a door open, he entered into an apartment the most delightful that ever was seen. There was in it a bed of cloth of gold, enriched with pearls, intermixed with rubies and emeralds; for by this time there appeared daylight sufficient for him to view and admire the magnificence of this sumptuous furniture. Having made fast the door, he composed himself for sleep. Next day he rose very early, and looking about on every side, he spied a painter's pal-

ette, with colors ready prepared and pencils. Re-
membering what the Princess had said to Abricotina
in regard to her own portrait, he immediately (for he
could paint as well as the most excellent masters)
seated himself before a mirror and drew his own
picture first. Then, in an oval, he painted that of the
Princess.

He had all her features so strong in his imagina-
tion that he had no occasion for her sitting. And as
his desire to please her had set him to work, never
did portrait bear a stronger resemblance. He had
painted himself upon one knee, holding the Princess' picture in one hand, and in the other a label
with this inscription, "She is better in my heart."

When the Princess went into her cabinet, she was
amazed to see the portrait of a man. And she fixed
her eyes upon it with so much the more surprise
because she also saw her own with it, and because
the words which were written upon the label af-
forded her ample room for curiosity. She persuaded
herself that it was Abricotina's doing; and all she
desired to know was whether the portrait was real or
imaginary. Rising in haste, she called Abricotina,
while the invisible Leander, with his little red cap,
slipped into the cabinet, impatient to know what
passed. The Princess bade Abricotina look upon the
picture and tell her what she thought of it.

After she had viewed it, "I insist," said she, " 'tis

the picture of that generous stranger to whom I am indebted for my life. Yes, yes, I am sure it is he; his very features, shape, and hair."

"Thou pretendest surprise," said the Princess, "but I know it was thou thyself who put it there."

"Who! I, madam?" replied Abricotina. "I protest I never saw the picture before in my life. Should I be so bold as to conceal from your knowledge a thing that so nearly concerns you? And by what miracle could I come by it? I never could paint, nor did any man ever enter this place; yet here he is painted with you."

"Some spirit, then, must have brought it hither," cried the Princess.

"How I tremble for fear, madam!" said Abricotina. "Was it not rather some lover? And therefore, if you will take my advice, let us burn it immediately."

" 'Twere a pity to burn it," cried the Princess, sighing; "a finer piece, methinks, cannot adorn my cabinet." And saying these words, she cast her eyes upon it. But Abricotina continued obstinate in her opinion that it ought to be burned, as a thing that could not come there but by the power of magic.

"And these words—'She is better in my heart,'" said the Princess; "must we burn them too?"

"No favor must be shown to anything," said Abricotina, "not even to your own portrait."

Abricotina ran away immediately for some fire,

while the Princess went to look out the window. Leander, unwilling to let his performance be burned, took this opportunity to convey it away without being perceived. He had hardly quitted the cabinet when the Princess turned about to look once more upon that enchanting picture, which had so delighted her. But how great was her surprise to find it gone! She sought for it all the room over; and Abricotina, returning, was no less surprised than her mistress; so that this last adventure put them both in the most terrible fright.

Leander took great delight in hearing and seeing his incomparable mistress; even though he had to eat every day at her table with the tabby cat, who fared never the worse for that. But his satisfaction was far from being complete, seeing he durst neither speak nor show himself; and he knew it was not a common thing for ladies to fall in love with persons invisible.

The Princess had a universal taste for amusement. One day, she was saying to her attendants that it would give her great pleasure to know how the ladies were dressed in all the courts of the universe. There needed no more words to send Leander all over the world. He wished himself in China, where he bought the richest stuffs he could lay his hands on, and got patterns of all the court fashions. From thence he flew to Siam, where he did the same. In three days he traveled over all the four parts of the world, and from time to time brought what he bought to the Palace of Calm Delights, and hid it all in a chamber, which he kept always locked.

When he had thus collected together all the rarities he could meet with—for he never wanted money, his rose always supplying him—he went and bought five or six dozen dolls, which he caused to be dressed in Paris, the place in the world where most regard is paid to fashions. They were all dressed differently, and as magnificently as could be, and Leander placed them all in the Princess' closet.

When she entered it, she was agreeably surprised to behold such a company of little mutes, every one decked with watches, bracelets, diamond buckles, or necklaces; and the most remarkable of them held a picture box in its hand, which the Princess, opening, found to contain Leander's portrait. She gave a loud shriek, and looking upon Abricotina, "There have appeared of late," said she, "so many wonders in this place that I know not what to think of them. My birds are all grown witty. I have only so much as to wish, but presently I have my desires. Twice have I now seen the portrait of him who rescued thee from the ruffians; and here are silks of all sorts, diamonds, embroideries, laces, and an infinite number of other rarities. What fairy is it that takes such care to pay me these agreeable civilities?"

Leander was overjoyed to hear and see her so much interested in his picture. Calling to mind that there was in a grotto which she often frequented a certain pedestal, on which a Diana, not yet finished, was to be erected, he resolved to place himself on this pedestal crowned with laurel, and holding a lyre in his hand, on which he played like another Apollo. He most anxiously waited the Princess' retiring to the grotto, which she did every day since her thoughts were so taken up with this unknown person. For what Abricotina had said, combined with the sight of the picture, had almost destroyed her repose. Her lively humor had changed into a pensive melancholy, and she grew ever fonder of solitude.

When she entered the grotto, she made a sign that nobody should follow her, so that her young damsels dispersed themselves into the neighboring walks. The Princess threw herself upon a bank of green turf, sighed, wept, and even talked, but so softly that Leander could not hear what she said. He had put his red cap on, that she might not see him at first. But having taken it off, she beheld him standing on the pedestal. At first she took him for a real statue, for he observed exactly the attitude in which he had placed himself, without moving so much as a finger.

She beheld with a kind of pleasure intermixed with fear, but pleasure soon dispelled her fear, and she continued to view the pleasing figure, which so exactly resembled life. The Prince, having tuned his lyre, began to play; whereupon the Princess, greatly surprised, could not resist the fear that seized her. She grew pale and fell into a swoon. Leander leaped from the pedestal, and putting on his little red cap, that he might not be perceived, took the Princess in his arms and gave her all the assistance that his zeal and tenderness could inspire. At length she opened her charming eyes and looked about in search of him, but she could perceive nobody. Yet she felt somebody who held her hands, kissed them, and bedewed them with his tears. It was a long time before she durst speak, and her spirits were in a confused agitation between fear and hope. She was afraid of the spirit, but loved the figure of the unknown. At length she said: "Courtly invisible, why are you not the person I desire you should be?" At these words Leander was going to declare himself, but durst not do it yet. "For," thought he, "if I again affright the object I adore and make her fear me, she will not love me." This consideration caused him to keep silence.

The Princess then, believing herself alone, called Abricotina and told her all the wonders of the animated statue; that it had played divinely, and that the invisible person had given her great assistance when she lay in a swoon.

"What pity 'tis," said she, "that this person should be so frightening, for nothing can be more amiable or acceptable than his behavior!"

"Who told you, madam," answered Abricotina, "that he is frightening? If he is the youth who saved me, he is beautiful as Cupid himself."

"If Cupid and the unknown are the same," replied the Princess, blushing, "I could be content to love Cupid. But alas! how far am I from such a happiness! I love a mere shadow; and this fatal picture joined to what thou hast told me have inspired me with inclinations so contrary to the precepts which I received from my mother that I am daily afraid of being punished for them."

"Oh! madam," said Abricotina, interrupting her, "have you not troubles enough already? Why should you anticipate afflictions which may never come to pass?"

It is easy to imagine what pleasure Leander took in this conversation.

In the meantime the little Furibon, still enamored of the Princess whom he had never seen, awaited with impatience the return of the four servants whom he had sent to the Island of Calm Delights. One of them at last came back, and after he had given the Prince a complete account of what had passed, told him that the island was defended by Amazons, and that unless he sent a very powerful army, it would be impossible to get into it. The King his father was dead, and Furibon was now lord of all. Disdaining, therefore, any opposition, he raised an army of four hundred thousand men, and put himself at the head of them, appearing like another Tom Thumb upon a war horse. Now, when the Amazons perceived his mighty host, they gave the Princess notice of it, who immediately dispatched her trusty Abricotina to the kingdom of the fairies, to beg her mother's instruction as to what she should do to drive the little Furibon from her territories. But Abricotina found the fairy in an angry humor.

"Nothing that my daughter does," said she, "escapes my knowledge. The Prince Leander is now in her palace. He loves her, and she has a tenderness for him. All my cares and precepts have not been able to guard her from the tyranny of love, and she is now under its fatal dominion. But it is the decree of destiny, and I must submit. Therefore, Abricotina, begone! Nor let me hear a word more of a daughter whose behavior has so much displeased me."

Abricotina returned with these ill tidings, whereat the Princess was almost distracted; and this was soon perceived by Leander, who was near her, though she could not see him. He beheld her grief with the greatest pain. However, he durst not then open his lips. But recollecting that Furibon was exceedingly covetous, he thought that, by giving him a sum of money, he might perhaps prevail upon him to retire. Thereupon, he dressed himself like an Amazon, and wished himself in the forest to catch his horse.

He had no sooner called him than Gris-de-line came leaping, prancing, and neighing for joy, for he was grown quite weary of being so long absent from his dear master. But when he beheld him dressed as a woman he hardly knew him. However, at the sound of his voice, he suffered the Prince to mount, and they soon arrived in the camp of Furibon, where Leander gave notice that a lady had come to speak with him from the Princess of Calm Delights. Immediately the little fellow put on his royal robes, and having placed himself upon his throne, he looked like a great toad counterfeiting a king.

Leander in his disguise of an Amazon harangued him, and told him that the Princess, preferring a quiet and peaceable life to the fatigues of war, had sent to offer his Majesty as much money as he pleased to demand, provided he would suffer her to continue in peace; but if he refused her proposal, she would omit no means that might serve for her defense. Furibon replied that he took pity on her, and would grant her the honor of his protection;

but that he demanded a hundred thousand millions
of pounds, and without which he would not return
to his kingdom. Leander answered that such a vast
sum would be too long a-counting, and therefore, if
he would say how many rooms he desired to have
filled with gold the Princess was generous and rich
enough to satisfy him.

Furibon was astonished to hear that, instead of
entreating, she would rather offer more. And it came
into his wicked mind to take all the money he could
get, and then seize the Amazon and kill her, so that
she could never return to her mistress. He told Leander, therefore, that he would have thirty chambers
of gold, all full to the ceiling. Leander, being conducted into the chambers, took his rose and shook
it, till every room was filled with all sorts of coin.
Furibon was in an ecstasy, and the more gold he
saw the greater was his desire to get hold of the
Amazon. So when all the rooms were full, he com-
manded his guards to seize her, alleging she had
brought him counterfeit money. Immediately Leander put on his little red cap and disappeared. The
guards, believing that the lady had escaped, ran
out and left Furibon alone. Leander, availing himself of the opportunity, took the tyrant by the hair,
and twisted his head off with the same ease he would
a pullet's; nor did the little wretch of a king see the
hand that killed him.

Leander, having secured his enemy's head, wished himself in the Palace of Calm Delights, where he found the Princess walking in the garden, sorrowfully considering the message which her mother had sent her, and planning means of repelling Furibon.

Suddenly she beheld a head hanging in the air, with nobody to hold it. This prodigy astonished her so greatly that she could not tell what to think of it. But her amazement increased when she saw the head laid at her feet, and heard a voice utter these words:

> "Charming Princess, cease your fear
> Of Furibon; whose head see here."

Abricotina, recognizing Leander's voice, cried: "I tell you, madam, the invisible person who speaks is the very stranger that rescued me."

The Princess seemed astonished, but yet pleased.

"Oh," said she, "if it be true that the invisible and the stranger are the same person, I confess I shall be glad to make him my acknowledgments."

Leander, still invisible, replied, "I will yet do more to deserve them." And so saying he returned to Furibon's army, where the report of the King's death had already spread throughout the camp. As soon as Leander appeared there in his usual habit, everybody knew him. All the officers and soldiers surrounded him, uttering the loudest acclamations of joy. In short, they acknowledged him for their king, and insisted that the crown by right belonged to him. For this he thanked them, and, as the first mark of his royal bounty, divided the thirty rooms of gold among the soldiers. This done, he returned to

his princess, after ordering his army to march back into his kingdom.

The Princess had gone to bed. Leander, therefore, retired into his own apartment, for he was very sleepy—so sleepy that he forgot to bolt his door. And so it happened that the Princess, rising early to taste the morning air, chanced to enter into this very chamber, and was astonished to find a young prince asleep upon the bed. She took a full view of him, and was convinced that he was the person whose picture she had in her diamond box.

"It is impossible," said she, "that this should be a spirit; for can spirits sleep? Is this a body composed of air and fire, without substance, as Abricotina told me?" She softly touched his hair, and heard him breathe, and looked at him as if she could have looked forever. While she was thus occupied, her mother, the fairy, entered with such a noise that Leander started out of his sleep.

But how deeply was he afflicted to behold his beloved Princess in the most deplorable condition! Her mother was dragging her by the hair and loading her with a thousand bitter reproaches. In what grief and consternation were the two young lovers, who saw themselves now upon the point of being separated forever! The Princess durst not open her lips, but cast her eyes upon Leander, as if to beg his assistance. He judged rightly that he ought not to deal rudely with a power superior to his own, and therefore he sought, by his eloquence and submission, to move the incensed fairy. He ran to her, threw himself at her feet, and besought her to have pity upon a young prince who would never change in his affection for her daughter.

The Princess, encouraged, also embraced her mother's knees, and declared that without Leander she could never be happy.

"Happy!" cried the fairy; "you know not the miseries of love nor the treacheries of which lovers are capable. They bewitch us only to poison our lives. I have known it by experience; and will you suffer the same?"

"Is there no exception, madam?" replied Leander, and his countenance showed him to be one.

But neither tears nor entreaties could move the implacable fairy. It is very probable that she would never have pardoned them had not the lovely Gentilla appeared at that instant in the chamber, more brilliant than the sun. Embracing the old fairy, she said:

"Dear sister, I am persuaded you cannot have forgotten the good office I did you when, after your unhappy marriage, you besought a readmittance into Fairyland. Since then I have never desired any favor at your hands, but now the time is come. Pardon, then, this lovely princess. Consent to her nuptials with this young prince. I will promise he shall be ever constant to her. The thread of their days shall be spun of gold and silk. They shall live to complete your happiness; and I will never forget the obligation you lay upon me."

"Charming Gentilla," cried the fairy, "I consent to whatever you desire. Come, my dear children, and receive my love." So saying, she embraced them both.

Abricotina, just then entering, cast her eyes upon Leander. She recognized him again, and saw that he was perfectly happy, and she, too, was quite satisfied.

"Prince," condescendingly said the fairy-mother, "I will remove the Island of Calm Delights into your

own kingdom, live with you myself, and do you great services."

Whether or not Prince Leander appreciated this offer, he bowed low, and assured his mother-in-law that no favor could be equal to the one he had that day received from her hands. This short compliment pleased the fairy exceedingly, for she belonged to those ancient days when people used to stand a whole day upon one leg complimenting one another. The nuptials were performed in a most splendid manner, and the young Prince and Princess lived together happily many years, beloved by everyone in the kingdom.

PRINCE
CHERRY

PRINCE CHERRY

LONG AGO THERE LIVED a monarch who was such a very honest man that his subjects entitled him the Good King. One day, when he was out hunting, a little white rabbit, which had been half killed by his hounds, leaped right into his Majesty's arms. Said he, caressing it: "This poor creature has put itself under my protection, and I will allow no one to injure it." So he carried it to his palace, had prepared for it a neat little rabbit hutch, with an abundance of the daintiest food, such as rabbits love, and there he left it.

That same night, when he was alone in his chamber, there appeared to him a beautiful lady. She was dressed neither in gold, nor silver, nor brocade; but her flowing robes were white as snow, and she wore a garland of white roses on her head. The Good King was greatly astonished at the sight; for his door was locked, and he wondered how so dazzling a lady could possibly enter. However, she soon removed his doubts.

"I am the fairy Candide," said she, with a smiling and gracious air. "Passing through the wood where you were hunting, I had a desire to know if you were as good as men say you are. I therefore changed myself into a white rabbit and took refuge in your arms. You saved me and now I know that those who are merciful to dumb beasts will be ten times more so to human beings. You merit the name your subjects give you: you are the Good King. I thank you for your protection, and shall be always one of your best friends. You have but to say what you most desire, and I promise you that your wish shall be granted."

"Madam," replied the King, "if you are a fairy, you must know, without my telling you, the wish of my heart. I have one well-beloved son, Prince Cherry. Whatever kindly feeling you have toward me, extend it to him."

"Willingly," said Candide. "I will make him the handsomest, richest, or most powerful prince in the world. Choose whatever you desire for him."

"None of the three," returned the father. "I wish him only to be good—the best prince in the whole world. Of what use would riches, power, or beauty be to him if he were a bad man?"

"You are right," said the fairy; "but I cannot make him good. He must be that of himself. I can only change his external fortunes. For his personal character, the utmost I can promise is to give him good counsel, reprove him for his faults, and even punish him, if he will not punish himself. You mortals can do the same with your children."

"Ah, yes!" said the King, sighing. Still, he felt that the kindness of a fairy was something gained for his son. Not long afterward the Good King died, contented and at peace.

Prince Cherry mourned deeply, for he dearly loved his father, and would have gladly given all his kingdoms and treasures to keep him in life a little longer. Two days after the Good King was no more, Prince Cherry was sleeping in his chamber when he saw the same dazzling vision which his father had seen. It was the fairy Candide.

"I promised your father," said she, "to be your best friend, and in pledge of this take what I now give you." And she placed a small gold ring upon his finger. "Poor as it looks, it is more precious than diamonds; for whenever you do ill it will prick your finger. If, after that warning, you still continue in evil, you will lose my friendship, and I shall become your direst enemy."

So saying, she disappeared, leaving Cherry in such amazement that he would have believed it all a dream save for the ring on his finger.

He was for a long time so good that the ring never

pricked him at all; and this made him so cheerful and pleasant in his humor that everybody called him "Happy Prince Cherry." But one unlucky day he was out hunting and found no sport, which vexed him so much that he showed his ill temper by his looks and ways. He fancied his ring felt very tight and uncomfortable, but as it did not prick him he took no heed of this. However, upon re-entering his

He saw reflected in the water his own frightful shape

palace, his little pet dog, Bibi, jumped up upon him and was sharply told to get away. The creature, accustomed to nothing but caresses, tried to attract his attention by pulling at his garments, whereupon Prince Cherry turned and gave it a severe kick. At this moment he felt in his finger a prick like a pin.

"What nonsense!" said he to himself. "The fairy must be making game of me. Why, what great evil have I done? I, the master of a great empire, cannot I kick my own dog?"

A voice replied, or else Prince Cherry imagined it: "No, sire; the master of a great empire has a right to do good, but not evil. I—a fairy—am as much above you as you are above your dog. I might punish you, kill you, if I chose; but I prefer leaving you to amend your ways. You have been guilty of three faults to-day—bad temper, passion, cruelty. See that you do better tomorrow."

The Prince promised, and kept his word for a while. But he had been brought up by a foolish nurse, who indulged him in every way and was always telling him that he would be a king one day, when he might do as he liked in all things. He found out now that even a king cannot always do as he wishes. It vexed him and made him angry. His ring began to prick him so often now that his little finger was continually bleeding. He disliked this, as was natural, and soon began to consider whether it

would not be easier to throw the ring away altogether rather than to be constantly annoyed by it.
It was such an unseemly thing for a king to have a
spot of blood on his finger! At last, unable to put up
with it any more, he took his ring off and hid it
where he would never see it again. He believed himself the happiest of men, for he could now do exactly
what he liked. But as he indulged his whim he became every day more and more miserable.

One day he saw a young girl, so beautiful that,
being always accustomed to have his own way, he
immediately determined to espouse her. He never
doubted that she would be only too glad to be made
a queen, for she was very poor. But Zelia—that was
her name—answered, to his great astonishment, that
she would rather not marry him.

"Do I displease you?" asked the Prince, into
whose mind it had never entered that he could displease anybody.

"Not at all, my Prince," said the honest peasant
maiden. "You are very handsome, very charming;
but you are not like your father the Good King. I
will not be your queen, for you would make me
miserable."

At these words the Prince's love seemed all to turn
into hatred. He gave orders to his guards to convey
Zelia to a prison near the palace, and then took

counsel with his foster brother, the one of all his ill companions who most incited him to do wrong.

"Sir," said this man, "if I were in your Majesty's place, I would never vex myself about a poor silly girl. Feed her on bread and water till she comes to her senses. And if she still refuses you, let her die in torment, as a warning to your other subjects should they venture to dispute your will. You will be disgraced should you suffer yourself to be mastered by a simple girl."

"But," said Prince Cherry, "shall I not be disgraced if I harm a creature so perfectly innocent?"

"No one is innocent who disputes your Majesty's authority," said the courtier, bowing; "and it is better to commit an injustice than allow it to be supposed you can ever be contradicted with impunity."

This touched Cherry on his weak point—his good impulses faded. He resolved once more to ask Zelia if she would marry him, and if she again refused, to sell her as a slave. Arrived at the cell in which she was confined, what was his astonishment to find her gone! He knew not whom to accuse, for he had kept the key in his pocket the whole time. At last, the foster brother suggested that the escape of Zelia might have been contrived by an old man, Suliman by name, the Prince's former tutor, who was the

only one who now ventured to blame him for anything that he did. Cherry sent immediately, and
ordered his old friend to be brought to him, loaded
heavily with irons. Then, full of fury, he went and
shut himself up in his own chamber, where he went
raging to and fro, till he was startled by a noise like
a clap of thunder. The fairy Candide stood before
him.

"Prince," said she, in a severe voice, "I promised
your father to give you good counsel and to punish
you if you refused to follow it. My counsel was forgotten, my punishment despised. Under the figure
of a man, you have become no better than the beasts
you chase: like a lion in fury, a wolf in gluttony, a
serpent in revenge, and a bull in brutality. Take,
therefore, in your new form the likeness of all these
animals."

Scarcely had Prince Cherry heard these words
than to his horror he found himself transformed into
what the fairy had named. He was a creature with
the head of a lion, the horns of a bull, the feet of a
wolf, and the tail of a serpent. At the same time he
felt himself transported to a distant forest, where,
standing on the bank of a stream, he saw reflected
in the water his own frightful shape, and heard a
voice saying:

"Look at thyself, and know that thy soul has become a thousand times uglier even than thy body."

Cherry recognized the voice of Candide, and in his rage would have sprung upon her and devoured her; but he saw nothing. The same voice behind him continued:

"Cease thy feeble fury, and learn to conquer thy pride by living in submission to thine own subjects."

Hearing no more, he soon quitted the stream, hoping at least to get rid of the sight of himself. But he had scarcely gone twenty paces when he tumbled into a pitfall that was laid to catch bears. The bear hunters, descending from some trees hard by, caught him, chained him, and only too delighted to get hold of such a curious-looking animal, led him along with them to the capital of his own kingdom.

There great rejoicings were taking place, and the bear hunters, asking what it was all about, were told that it was because Prince Cherry, the torment of his subjects, had just been struck dead by a thunderbolt—just punishment of all his crimes. Four courtiers, his wicked companions, had wished to divide his throne between them; but the people had risen up against them and offered the crown to Suliman, the old tutor whom Cherry had ordered to be arrested.

All this the poor monster heard. He even saw Suliman sitting upon his own throne and trying to calm the populace by representing to them that it was not certain Prince Cherry was dead; that he might return one day to reassume with honor the crown which Suliman only consented to wear as a sort of viceroy.

"I know his heart," said the honest and faithful old man; "it is tainted, but not corrupt. If alive, he may reform yet, and be his father all over again to you, his people, whom he has caused to suffer so much."

These words touched the poor beast so deeply that he ceased to beat himself against the iron bars of the cage in which the hunters carried him about. He became gentle as a lamb, and suffered himself to be taken quietly to a menagerie, where were kept all sorts of strange and ferocious animals—a place which he had himself often visited as a boy, but had never thought he should be shut up there himself one day.

However, he owned he had deserved it all, and began to make amends by showing himself very obedient to his keeper. This man was almost as great a brute as the animals he had charge of, and when he was in ill humor he used to beat them without rhyme or reason. One day, while he was sleeping, a tiger broke loose and leaped upon him, eager to devour him. Cherry at first felt a thrill of pleasure at the thought of being revenged. Then, seeing how helpless the man was, he wished himself free, that he might defend him. Immediately the doors of his cage opened. The keeper, waking up, saw the strange beast leap out, and imagined, of course, that he was going to be slain at once. Instead, he saw the tiger lying dead, and the strange beast creeping up and laying itself at his feet to be caressed. But as he lifted up his hand to stroke it, a voice was heard say-

ing, "Good actions never go unrewarded." And instead of the frightful monster, there crouched on the ground a pretty little dog.

Cherry, delighted to find himself thus metamorphosed, caressed the keeper in every possible way, till at last the man took him up into his arms and carried him to the King, to whom he related this wonderful story, from beginning to end. The Queen wished to have the charming little dog; and Cherry would have been exceedingly happy could he have forgotten that he was originally a man and a king. He was lodged most elegantly, had the richest of collars to adorn his neck, and heard himself praised continually. But his beauty rather brought him into trouble, for the Queen, afraid lest he might grow too large for a pet, took the advice of the veterinarians, who ordered that he should be fed entirely upon bread, and that very sparingly. So poor Cherry was sometimes nearly starved.

One day, when they gave him his crust for breakfast, a fancy seized him to go and eat it in the palace garden. So he took the bread in his mouth and trotted away toward a stream which he knew, and where he sometimes stopped to drink. But instead of the stream he saw a splendid palace, glittering with gold and precious stones. Entering the doors was a crowd of men and women, magnificently dressed. And within there was singing and dancing and good cheer of all sorts. Yet, however grandly and gaily the people went in, Cherry noticed that those who came out were pale, thin, ragged, half naked, and covered with wounds and sores. Some of them dropped dead at once. Others dragged themselves on a little way and then lay down, dying of hunger, and vainly begging a morsel of bread from others who were entering—who never took the least notice of them.

Cherry perceived one woman, who was trying feebly to gather and eat some green herbs. "Poor thing!" said he to himself; "I know what it is to be hungry, and I want my breakfast badly enough. But it won't kill me to wait till dinnertime, and my crust may save the life of this poor woman."

So the little dog ran up to her and dropped his bread at her feet. She picked it up and ate it with avidity. Soon she looked quite recovered, and Cherry, delighted, was trotting back again to his kennel when he heard loud cries, and saw a young girl dragged by four men to the door of the palace, which they were trying to compel her to enter. Oh, how he wished himself a monster again, as when he slew the tiger!—for the young girl was none other than his beloved Zelia. Alas! what could a poor little dog do to defend her? But he ran forward and barked at the men, and bit their heels, until at last they chased him away with heavy blows. And then he lay down outside the palace door, determined to watch and see what had become of Zelia.

Conscience pricked him now. "What!" thought he, "I am furious against these wicked men, who are carrying her away; and did I not do the same myself? Did I not cast her into prison, and intend to sell her as a slave? Who knows how much more wickedness I might not have done to her and others, if Heaven's justice had not stopped me in time?"

While he lay thinking and repenting, he heard a window open and saw Zelia throw out of it a bit of dainty meat. Cherry, who felt hungry enough by this time, was just about to eat it, when the woman to whom he had given his crust snatched him up in her arms.

"Poor little beast!" cried she, patting him, "every bit of food in that palace is poisoned: you shall not touch a morsel."

At the same time the voice in the air repeated again, "Good actions never go unrewarded." And Cherry found himself changed into a beautiful little white pigeon. He remembered with joy that white was the color of the fairy Candide, and began to hope that she was taking him into favor again.

So he stretched his wings, delighted that he might now have a chance of approaching his fair Zelia. He flew up to the palace windows, and, finding one of them open, entered and sought everywhere, but he could not find Zelia. Then, in despair, he flew out again, resolved to go over the world until he beheld her once more.

He took flight at once and traversed many countries, as swiftly as a bird can, but found no trace of his beloved. At length in a desert, sitting beside an old hermit in his cave and partaking with him his frugal repast, Cherry saw a poor peasant girl and recognized Zelia. Transported with joy, he flew in, perched on her shoulder, and expressed his delight and affection by a thousand caresses.

She, charmed with the pretty little pigeon, caressed it in her turn, and promised it that if it would stay with her she would love it always.

"What have you done, Zelia?" said the hermit, smiling. And while he spoke the white pigeon vanished, and there stood Prince Cherry in his own natural form. "Your enchantment ended, Prince, when Zelia promised to love you. Indeed, she has loved you always, but your many faults constrained her to hide her love. These are now amended, and you may both live happy if you will, because your union is founded upon mutual esteem."

Cherry and Zelia threw themselves at the feet of the hermit, whose form also began to change. His soiled garments became of dazzling whiteness, and his long beard and withered face grew into the flowing hair and lovely countenance of the fairy Candide.

"Rise up, my children," said she; "I must now transport you to your palace and restore to Prince Cherry his father's crown, of which he is now worthy."

She had scarcely ceased speaking when they found themselves in the chamber of Suliman, who, delighted to find again his beloved pupil and master, willingly resigned the throne, and became the most faithful of his subjects.

King Cherry and Queen Zelia reigned together for many years, and it is said that the former was so blameless and strict in all his duties that, though he constantly wore the ring which Candide had restored to him, it never once pricked his finger enough to make it bleed.

THE PRINCE
WITH THE NOSE

THE PRINCE WITH
THE NOSE

THERE WAS ONCE a king who was pas-
sionately in love with a beautiful princess,
but she could not be married because a
magician had enchanted her. The King
went to a good fairy to inquire what he should do.
Said the fairy, after receiving him graciously: "Sir,
I will tell you a great secret. The Princess has a great
cat whom she loves so well that she cares for nothing
and nobody else. But she will be obliged to marry
any person who is adroit enough to walk upon the
cat's tail."

"That will not be very difficult," thought the King
to himself, and departed, resolving to trample the
cat's tail to pieces if necessary. He went immediately
to the palace of his fair mistress and the cat. The

animal came in front of him, arching its back in
anger as it was wont to do. The King lifted up his
foot, thinking nothing would be so easy as to tread
on the tail, but he found himself mistaken. Minon—
that was the creature's name—twisted itself round so

sharply that the King only hurt his own foot by
stamping on the floor. For eight days did he pursue
the cat everywhere. Up and down the palace halls
he was after it from morning till night, but with no
better success. The tail seemed made of quicksilver,
so very lively was it. At last the King had the good

fortune to catch Minon sleeping, when tramp! tramp! he trod on the tail with all his force.

Minon woke up, mewed horribly, and immediately changed from a cat into a large, fierce-looking man, who regarded the King with flashing eyes.

"You must marry the Princess," cried he, "because you have broken the enchantment in which I held her; but I will be revenged on you. You shall have a son with a nose as long as—that"; he made in the air a curve of half a foot; "yet he shall believe it is just like all other noses, and shall be always unfortunate till he has found out it is not. And if you ever tell anybody of this threat of mine, you shall die on the spot." So saying, the magician disappeared.

The King, who was at first much terrified, soon began to laugh at this adventure. "My son might have a worse misfortune than to have too long a nose," thought he. "At least it will hinder him neither in seeing nor in hearing. I will go and find the Princess and marry her at once."

He did so, but he lived only a few months longer, and died before his little son was born, so that nobody knew anything about the secret of the nose.

The little Prince was so much wished for that when he came into the world they agreed to call him Prince Wish. He had beautiful blue eyes and a sweet little mouth, but his nose was so big that it covered half his face. The Queen his mother was inconsolable. But her ladies tried to satisfy her by telling her that the nose was not nearly as large as it seemed, that it would grow smaller as the Prince grew bigger, and that if it did not a large nose was indispensable to a hero. All great soldiers, they said, had great noses, as everybody knew. The Queen was so very fond of her son that she listened eagerly to all these comforting words. In time she grew so used to the Prince's nose that it did not seem to her any larger than ordinary noses of the court; where, in process of time, everybody with a long nose became very much admired, and the unfortunate people who had only snubs received very little attention.

Great care was observed in the education of the Prince; and as soon as he could speak they told him all sorts of amusing tales, in which all the bad people had short noses, and all the good people had long ones. No person was suffered to come near him who had not a nose of more than ordinary length. Nay, to such an extent did the courtiers carry their fancy that the noses of all the little babies were ordered to be pulled out as far as possible several times a day, in order to make them grow. But grow as they would, they never could grow as long as that of Prince Wish.

When he was old enough his tutor taught him history; and whenever any great king or lovely

princess was referred to, the tutor always took care
to mention that he or she had a long nose. All the
royal apartments were filled with pictures and por-
traits having this peculiarity, so that at last Prince
Wish began to regard the length of his nose as his
greatest perfection, and would not have had it an
inch less even to save his crown.

When he was twenty years old his mother and
his people wished him to marry. They procured for
him the likenesses of many princesses, but the one he
preferred was Princess Darling, daughter of a powerful monarch and heiress to several kingdoms. Alas!
with all her beauty, this Princess had one great misfortune, a little turned-up nose, which, everyone
else said, made her only the more bewitching. But
here, in the kingdom of Prince Wish, the courtiers
were thrown by it into the utmost perplexity. They
were in the habit of laughing at all small noses; but
how dared they make fun of the nose of Princess
Darling? Two unfortunate gentlemen, whom Prince
Wish had overheard doing so, were ignominiously
banished from the court and capital.

After this, the courtiers became alarmed, and
tried to correct their habit of speech. But they would
have found themselves in constant difficulties had
not one clever person hit upon a bright idea. He said
that, though it was indispensably necessary for a man
to have a great nose, women were entirely different;

and that a learned man had discovered in a very old manuscript that the clebrated Cleopatra, Queen of Egypt, the beauty of the ancient world, had a turned-up nose. With this information Prince Wish was so delighted that he made the courtier a very handsome present, and immediately sent off ambassadors to demand Princess Darling in marriage.

She accepted his offer at once, and returned with the ambassadors. He made all haste to meet and welcome her, but when she was only three leagues distant from his capital, before he had time even to kiss her hand, the magician who had once assumed the shape of his mother's cat, Minon, appeared in the air and carried her off before the lover's very eyes.

Prince Wish, almost beside himself with grief, declared that nothing could induce him to return to his throne and kingdom till he had found Darling. He would suffer none of his courtiers or attendants to follow him; but bidding them all adieu, mounted a good horse, laid the reins on the animal's neck, and let him take him wherever he would.

The horse entered a wide-extended plain, and trotted on steadily the whole day without passing a single house. Master and beast began almost to faint with hunger. And Prince Wish might have wished himself at home again had he not discovered, just at dusk, a cavern, where there sat, beside

a bright lantern, a little woman who might have
been a hundred or more years old.

She put on her spectacles the better to look at the
stranger, and he noticed that her nose was so small
that the spectacles would hardly stay on it. Then the

Prince and the fairy—for she was a fairy—burst into
laughter.

"What a funny nose!" cried the one.

"Not so funny as yours, madam," returned the
other. "But pray let us leave our noses alone, and be

good enough to give me something to eat, for I am dying with hunger, and so is my poor horse."

"With all my heart," answered the fairy. "Although your nose is ridiculously long, you are no less the son of one of my best friends. I loved your father like a brother. He had a very handsome nose."

"What is wanting in my nose?" asked Wish, rather savagely.

"Oh! nothing at all. On the contrary, there is a great deal too much of it. But never mind, one may be a very honest man, and yet have too big a nose. As I said, I was a great friend of your father's; he came often to see me. I was very pretty then, and oftentimes he used to say to me, 'My sister—'"

"I will hear the rest, madam, with pleasure, when I have supped. But will you condescend to remember that I have tasted nothing all day?"

"Poor boy," said the fairy, "I will give you some supper directly. And while you eat it I will tell you my history in six words, for I hate much talking. A long tongue is as insupportable as a long nose. I remember when I was young how much I used to be admired because I was not a talker. Indeed, someone said to the Queen my mother—for poor as you see me now, I am the daughter of a great king, who always—"

"Ate when he was hungry, I hope," interrupted the Prince, whose patience was fast departing.

"You are right," said the imperturbable old fairy; "and I will bring you your supper directly, only I wish first just to say that the King my father—"

"Hang the King your father!" Prince Wish was about to exclaim, but he stopped himself, and only observed that, however much the pleasure of her conversation might make him forget his hunger, it could not have the same effect upon his horse, who was really starving.

The fairy, pleased with his civility, called her servants and bade them supply him at once with all he needed. "And," added she, "I must say you are very polite and very good-tempered, in spite of your nose."

"What has the old woman to do with my nose?" thought the Prince. "If I were not so very hungry, I would soon show her what she is—a regular old gossip and chatterbox. And she fancies herself to be quiet! One must be very foolish not to know one's own defects. This comes of being born a princess. Flatterers have spoiled her and persuaded her that she talks little. Little, indeed! I never knew anybody to chatter so much."

While the Prince thus meditated, the servants were laying the table, the fairy asking them a hundred unnecessary questions, simply for the pleasure of hearing herself talk. "Well," thought Wish, "I am delighted that I came hither, if only to learn how

wise I have been in never listening to flatterers, who
hide from us our faults, or make us believe they are
perfections. But they could never deceive me. I
know all my own weak points, I trust." As truly he
believed he did.

So he went on eating contentedly, nor stopped
till the old fairy began to address him.

"Prince," said she, "will you be kind enough to
turn a little? Your nose casts such a shadow that I
cannot see what is on my plate. And, as I was saying,
your father admired me and always made me welcome at court. What is the court etiquette there
now? Do the ladies still go to assemblies, prome-
nades, balls?—I beg your pardon for laughing, but
how very long your nose is."

"I wish you would cease to speak of my nose,"
said the Prince, becoming annoyed. "It is what it is,
and I do not desire it any shorter."

"Oh! I see that I have vexed you," returned the
fairy. "Nevertheless, I am one of your best friends,
and so I shall take the liberty of always—" She would
doubtless have gone on talking till midnight; but the
Prince, unable to bear it any longer, here interrupted
her, thanked her for her hospitality, bade her a hasty
adieu, and rode away.

He traveled for a long time, half over the world,
but he heard no news of Princess Darling. However,
in each place he visited, he heard one remarkable

fact—the great length of his own nose. The little boys
in the streets jeered at him, the peasants stared at
him, and the more polite ladies and gentlemen
whom he met in society used to try in vain to keep
from laughing, and to get out of his way as soon as
they could. So the poor Prince became gradually
quite forlorn and solitary. He thought all the world
was mad, but still he never thought of there being
anything queer about his own nose.

At last the old fairy, who, though she was a chatterbox, was very good-natured, saw that he was almost breaking his heart. She felt sorry for him and
wished to help him in spite of himself, for she knew
the enchantment which hid from him the Princess
Darling could never be broken till he had discovered
his own defect. So she went in search of the Princess,
and being more powerful than the magician, since
she was a good fairy and he was an evil magician,
she got her away from him and shut up the Princess
in a palace of crystal, which she placed on the road
which Prince Wish had to travel.

He was riding along, very melancholy, when he
saw the palace. At its entrance was a room, made of
the purest glass, in which sat his beloved princess,
as smiling and beautiful as ever. He leaped from his
horse and ran toward her. She held out her hand for
him to kiss, but he could not get at it for the glass.
Transported with eagerness and delight, he dashed

his sword through the crystal and succeeded in breaking a small opening, to which she put up her beautiful rosy mouth. But it was in vain; Prince Wish could not approach it. He twisted his neck about, and turned his head in all directions, till at length, putting up his hand to his face, he discovered the impediment.

"It must be confessed," exclaimed he, "that my nose is too long."

At that moment the glass walls all split asunder, and the old fairy appeared, leading Princess Darling.

"Avow, Prince," said she, "that you are very much obliged to me, for now the enchantment is ended. You may marry the object of your choice. But," added she, smiling, "I fear I might have talked to you forever on the subject of your nose, and you would not have believed me regarding its length till it became an obstacle to your own inclinations. Now behold it!" and she held up a crystal mirror. "Are you satisfied to be no different from other people?"

"Perfectly," said Prince Wish, who found his nose had shrunk to an ordinary length. And taking the Princess Darling by the hand, he kissed her courteously, affectionately, and warmly. Then they departed to their own country, and lived very happily all their days.

THE BEAUTIFUL
Illustrated Junior Library
EDITIONS